KIVA

KIVA

A Novel

Ronald K. Wetherington

SANTA FE

Sunstone books may be purchased for educational, business, or sales promotional use.
For information please write: Special Markets Department, Sunstone Press,
P.O. Box 2321, Santa Fe, New Mexico 87504-2321.

Cover image by Jack Brauer
Book design › Vicki Ahl
Body typeface › Trebuchet MS
Printed on acid-free paper
∞
eBook 978-1-61139-230-2

Library of Congress Cataloging-in-Publication Data

Wetherington, Ronald K.
  Kiva : a novel / by Ronald K. Wetherington.
      pages cm
  ISBN 978-0-86534-975-9 (softcover : alk. paper)
  1. Kivas--Fiction. 2. Indians of North America--Antiquities--Fiction. 3. Excavations (Archaeology)--New Mexico--Fiction. 4. Women archaeologists--Fiction.
5. Graduate teaching assistants--Fiction. 6. Murder--Investigation--Fiction.
I. Title.
  PS3623.E884K58 2013
  813'.6--dc23

                                        2013038249

WWW.SUNSTONEPRESS.COM
SUNSTONE PRESS / POST OFFICE BOX 2321 / SANTA FE, NM 87504-2321 /USA
(505) 988-4418 / ORDERS ONLY (800) 243-5644 / FAX (505) 988-1025

For Adam,
sojourner across myth and reality.

Preface

One writes best about what one already knows, so almost all of the setting in this novel is factual. Fort Burgwin—a 19th Century military post—has been excavated and restored over the past 50+ years and has served as a research center and campus of Southern Methodist University since the 1960s. Pot Creek Pueblo, ancestral home to the Northern and Southern Tiwa speakers, lies on the 300-acre site of the Center. I began excavating it in 1958 as an undergraduate student at Texas Tech under the direction of Dr. Fred Wendorf, and it subsequently became my doctoral dissertation at the University of Michigan.

The room block noted in the narrative does indeed exist, but I have relocated it, and the specific rooms and underlying kiva that focus the story are fictional. Kivas do, however, underlie some of the more recent room blocks as either earlier occupations or replaced and remodeled structures, due to the century-long occupation of the pueblo.

The masked figure potsherd was actually recovered at the site and possibly indicates the presence of the kachina cult in the northern pueblos, as well as an underlying clan organization of some sort, both of which disappeared over time. The earlier enmity between Taos and Picuris—both of whose ancestors lived at Pot Creek—is actually reflected in the tale of the Taos scalp in the Picuris scalp house, but such enmity is long passed. Belief in ghosts, however, permeates the folktales of northern New Mexico, among Hispanic and Indian peoples alike.

While it is hypothesized that sociopolitical discord prompted the exodus and redistribution of Pot Creek's occupants, there is no evidence of any Aztec presence, or even influence, here.

The characters, of course, do not represent any actual individuals, living or dead.

Prologue

In the old days close to three hundred families had lived here—nearly fifteen hundred souls counting the children—and the glistening adobe rooms were stacked three high in some places. You could stand on the topmost roof and see the world; see beyond the pueblo to the nearby cornfields and the surrounding forest. If you listened carefully at night you could sometimes hear the nearer of the two creeks, and in the daytime you could follow the line of willows and cottonwoods as they marked the meandering stream banks off into the distance.

Here at this highest point of the pueblo the world was clearly defined: the abruptly rising hills cupped the narrow valley east and west, and the high pass in the distance gave the view south a visual boundary. To the north where the converged rivers spilled out onto the vast plateau, the valley's end—obscured by the hills and terraces—was marked in the sky: like the people of the valley back then, its clouds seldom had occasion to venture beyond it, and as they did they dissipated.

But those were the old days, and now the people were dissipating like the clouds did. Those remaining numbered scarcely more than fifty—occupying only two of the nine clustered multistory room blocks. The other six clans had moved away, steadily over the past ten years, some going north to build a new pueblo near their ancestral home, and others south to another valley fed by waters flowing from another sacred mountain.

Those remaining would soon leave, as well. The strength of numbers needed to keep up with repairs and till the land and hunt and initiate the young into the clan's kiva society was now below the critical mass, and it was a struggle. So the pueblo had already begun to lose its luster. The abandoned room blocks were sealed up and it was no longer safe to climb the ladders to the high point and talk to the world and listen.

They had remained, this small tenacious group, in a dwindling hope of setting things right once again—of tidying up the past by expiation or prayer or ceremony so that the pueblo, when finally abandoned, would not know evil as it had in the past. Things, not just people, have life and death as part of their cycles. Places, like persons, can be good and evil, and sometimes places can be more dangerous than people. So remedies are always sought to set things right and restore a kind of harmony between place and people. This was the mission and hope of these last few.

They would leave, also, and very soon. Their clan would join the others. Through the long passage of time, their clans would disappear and their languages would change and where there was one group originally—here in this place—there would later become four and these would become part of history. Two of these, the Taos and Picuris villages, would remain close to their original home. The other two, the peoples of Sandia and Isleta, would move south to Albuquerque, close to their ancestors' original home. And yet, the original home of all was in the water and under the mountain and beneath the lake and in still other places where history can never take us because the record is not written.

Eventually, through the long passage of time, this place would be rediscovered. Not by descendants with remnants of memory for their ancestors here, but by archeologists with some skill in piecing together the connection between then and now. Masters of snatching the unknown from the known, the archeologists would come into this narrow valley and empty out its mysteries. Or try.

◊◊◊

Societies that preserve written records of the past have some advantage over those that don't. The advantage lies in our Western persuasion that history interpreted as it happened is more precise and accurate and objective than a reconstruction of the past which depends only on oral tradition.

On the other hand, societies with only oral passages to the past leave artifacts for interpreting that past, and piecing together the sundry shards of those yesterdays is the work of the archeologist. Artifacts, of course, don't speak for themselves. They often offer some tempting mixture of myth and reality. Stitching these together without necessarily making the distinction is compelling reading.

This brings us to the pages that follow. There are pieces of both history and prehistory in them, sprinkled with doses of educated guess. There are also patches of myth and reality, not distinguished because they cannot be. This is the story—more precisely, a story—of what happened in this pueblo and why it happened and the role that an archeologist played in revealing it. More critically, it is the dual story of how the past influences the present and how the present can influence the past.

Weaving them together can be risky. The oral tradition of prehistory and of non-written history is always selective: it preserves the central and the sacred in life, releasing the peripheral and nonessential. History and the oral tradition are therefore not equivalent—nor always compatible. Some tales are better imagined than revealed, some histories better reserved in myth than preserved in scholarship. All stories are true, it is said; some of them actually happened.

So there are two stories here, or one story told twice.

1

Thinking back, it was not difficult to identify the particular turning point when things began to go wrong. At the time, of course, no event so absent of motive could have been seen as an omen. Neither was there warning within the subsequent events as they innocently unfolded, slowly and without obvious connection. So that by the time Graciella became aware of the dangerous direction things had taken it was far too late to stop them. Even if she could, or if she wanted to.

And so it became a curious obsession for her, to discover what connections there were among those events and what role her imagination was playing and whether she was truly sane or whether the perceived danger was a loose-fitting fabric sheltering a deeper madness. Now, after fourteen months, she had to find out and had returned—was drawn to?—that original turning point again: that ancient pueblo room with its center-post and basin, once excavated and so many months now sealed with plastic and back-filled with excavated dirt to protect it.

Three other rooms like it had been excavated that season—four in all, aligned in a row—but it had happened in this one, whose floor now lay exactly eighty centimeters below where she stood, shovel in hand. Waiting in expectation, she thought? Did the room know? Could she now sense an almost tangible force, pulling downward? Or was it simply (and more likely) her expectation mixed with apprehension, both growing keener as the room floor grew closer?

Moth to flame: the analogy briefly fluttered across her mind and she dismissed it as she recalled once more that initial event. Now more vivid in her recollection as the room itself took on more of its familiar form, it had been late June of last year on a day even hotter than today.

It was her second season in Taos, this time as a graduate teaching assistant in the Archeological Field School rather than as an enrolled student.

Greg Parson had thought enough of her skills and dedication to give her one of the three TA assignments. Marcie Wells and Derek Rowan were the other two. Marcie was given the responsibility of overseeing the cataloging, while Derek and Graciella supervised two teams of students in the field excavations. Graciella took Rooms 703 and 704 of the Unit VII room-block and had four students assigned to her. These rooms were at the top of the mound, and thus represented the center of the once multi-storied architectural unit. Since all upper rooms had fallen in, rooms at the center normally had upper floor debris which had fallen into and then piled on top of the ground-floor rooms. Rooms 703 and 704 were such rooms.

It was in their second week. Two of the four rooms—701 and 703—had been excavated and all upper floor debris screened to within 10 centimeters of the floor. A block of room fill had been left unexcavated in each room in order to profile and interpret the pattern of collapse and to determine the number of upper floors. The block in Room 703 had been drawn and interpreted, and Greg had given the okay for its removal. Room 704 was still almost a meter from floor, and Graciella had assigned two students inside the room, another on the screen, and the fourth to carry buckets of fill from room to screen. Graciella concentrated on doing the final trowel work on the floor in 703 by herself.

Excavation had earlier revealed the common basin with center post feature, but these had remained covered until the profile block was removed. When it happened, Graciella was clearing the last of the fill from the basin—a shallow circular depression, 45 cm. in diameter, rimmed with a raised adobe curb. It lay in the center of the 2 by 3 meter room. In the center of the basin was a posthole 12 cm.—almost 4-1/2 inches—in diameter, with remains of a juniper post still in place.

Burned corn kernels partially filled the basin, along with fragments of burned adobe. The post and portions of the adobe floor and walls had been burned, but the pattern was not uniform. This commonly indicated that the room had burned after having been abandoned and collapsed, hence partially protected from fire by fallen floor and wall fragments from above. Here at the center of the room block, there had been two floors above, well defined in the room fill profile.

It had happened as she toweled the last of the burned corn into a sample bag. First was a subtle cooling sensation on her trowel hand. Curious, she had lifted her hand. Had she imagined this? She then felt it on her face, this time a distinct caress of cold air. Startled, she abruptly sat up and looked around. Outside the room, all was still. In the adjacent rooms, students worked quietly, and Graciella could hear the occasional scrape of shovels. Beyond, strains of music from a radio hung heavy in the stillness. The sun was oppressive, the heat relentless, not even dust motes were moving.

And now a strong gust of chilled air assaulted her face, forceful enough to displace the drooping strands of hair on her forehead and cool the tracks of sweat coursing down her cheeks. Did a subtle whistle accompany this? She was certain she had heard it. She drew her face closer to the floor in an attempt to determine the source of this air, which apparently came from the basin itself. But it disappeared, this sensation, as abruptly as it had come.

Graciella remained still a moment, glancing around to see whether anyone had seen or felt or heard anything, but the world outside Room 703 was unconcerned and unchanged. She then concluded that it might have been something imagined. One occasionally gets a chill, she reasoned, at unexpected times. Hunched down with her trowel, she had likely suffered a brief loss of circulation. Constricted peripheral blood flow. Light-headedness from heat exhaustion. She tried to forget the entire matter.

She had worked in the room for another hour or so, carefully profiling the four walls using a line-level and string, in order to determine where the floor and walls might be slumping. This would help identify any underlying structure. There was a slight downward slope to the northeast, and Graciella had pointed this out to Greg, who had said, okay, next season you can dig this kiva underneath 703. And that was all of it. For a while.

Brought out of her reverie by a magpie's raking call, Graciella now wiped a streak of dusty sweat from her forehead. The rumble of thunder over a distant mountain caused her to squint up at the eastern horizon. The sun was white and hot at this elevation, just under 7,500 feet, but the early afternoon breeze now signaled the approach, on schedule, of rain-bearing clouds from the eastern rise.

Graciella looked at her watch. Almost three o'clock. Cumulus clouds building up over the ridge would bring stronger winds within the hour, then release a brief but heavy downpour here before dissipating west across the narrow valley. The adjacent valley was much more arid. A rain shadow in text-book perfection, Graciella thought. Well, okay. She would stop for today. Even a short rain would transform the dry backfill into a muddy quagmire.

She measured the depth with her tape, noted the measurement in her field notebook, and laid the shovel in the center of the excavated square. The sheet of black plastic was in place well before the rain. Covering the excavation at a slight vertical angle permitting most water to run off instead of into the open square, the plastic was now outlined with stone cobbles, weighting it down to keep it safe from assailing winds until tomorrow. Tomorrow she would finish this work and revisit the room she had briefly known once before.

Large, heavy drops began to pattern the hood and windshield of her Explorer as she got in, etching serrated circles in the dusty patina. She decided to sit for a while instead of returning to camp. She inhaled deeply. The first raindrops had released the captive aromas of the land, and she rolled down the window part way. The combination of earth, juniper, and sage odors were strong and harmonizing, and with the sound of the rain created a restful moment.

Graciella shut her eyes and rested her head against the seat back as she savored the bouquet and its individual scents. How ironic, after all that had happened, that she now consciously identified the two aromatic components of sage and juniper in the freshening rain. Before the turn of events, she had never found the pungent odors worthy of more than casual notice; now they were remarkable in their significance. In further irony, the scents in fact came from neither true juniper nor true sage, yet the aromatic oils producing these odors were organically identical to those of their namesakes. She smiled to herself. Naming the aromas did not name the sources, so what does that tell us?

She started the engine, shifted into reverse to back onto the narrow dirt road, and followed it out, trying to avoid the deep ruts which were now rivulets. It tells us, she thought, that significance does not increase with sci-entific accuracy, and that taxonomies serve narrow purposes. *Artemesia* and *estafiata* give the same sage different meanings in their respective cultures. If I were Aztec, my herbal would identify it as *Iztauyattl*. Would it clear fever and soothe throats in all taxonomies, she wondered? Probably, she thought, but it would only call spirits in a few. Only one, perhaps. Spirits from a single, ancient pueblo culture. She recalled again the dream—more than a dream—that had, with these aromas, sent her on this new trajectory a year ago, so shortly after the event in Room 703 and now so obviously connected to that event.

She jerked the wheel violently to the left, avoiding a rain-filled pothole of unremembered depth, and down-shifted as she approached a sharp turn beyond a large juniper. And <u>that</u>, she almost said aloud, is why these aromas are no longer transparent to me. Part of her, she knew, wished that they were. "Damn!" she said. "Will it finally end, tomorrow?" Her grip on the wheel tightened, only partly due to the road conditions.

2

Her field camp was only a quarter-mile away, across New Mexico Highway 518 that separated the narrow valley, south of Ranchos de Taos. The camp was actually a reconstructed fort from the 1850s, Cantonment Burgwin, which now—as the Ft. Burgwin Research Center—housed living quarters, library, computer facilities, offices, classrooms and laboratories for both research and teaching.

It was still raining, though not as hard, when she approached the Officers Quarters at the west end of the parade ground. She was billeted in one of the efficiency apartments. As it was late August, the summer classes were over. Only one other person, Ned Aberle, a geologist, was in the five-apartment complex—he occupied an efficiency apartment across the hall—and the Center's Director and his wife, living in the Commander's Quarters at the other end of the parade ground, were the only other scientists currently in residence.

Graciella parked in the small gravel lot and threw a poncho over her head as she got out of the Explorer. She scurried into the apartment, hung up the poncho, and put her field notebook on the desk next to her computer. On the wall opposite the desk, under the other window in the room, was a single bed. A narrow table which doubled as a repository of books and notes as well as a dining surface lay against the windowless wall. On the opposite wall were a small kitchenette and a doorway leading to the bath.

The clouds and rain obscured the sunlight and Graciella opened the shutters on the window by the desk and turned on the desk lamp. A light staccato knock came from the door. "Come in, Ned," she said, sitting on the bed and removing her boots. Not likely to be anyone else.

"Did you get much done before the rain?" Ned Aberle was a lanky young man of twenty-seven with sandy hair that reminded Graciella of a young Art

Garfunkel, though it was not as golden and not quite as curly. He had a narrow face with an angular jaw and high-bridged, slightly beaked nose. He wore rimless glasses and carried two longneck beers.

"A meter and twenty centimeters," Graciella answered him, taking a beer from his extended hand. "Thanks." She sat on the bed, motioning him to the desk chair. He was writing a field report from his just-completed graduate field school, focused on the geological history of this narrow valley. He would be finished and gone in another week.

"That's quite a lot. Watch you don't get heat stroke, Grace."

She smiled briefly at the name, Grace, although it was her given name and she had only begun using Graciella since the recent events. She had encouraged but not pressed her friends to use it. Ned had preferred to stick to "Grace", perhaps self-conscious about "Graciella" or just out of habit. Her explanation that it was the familiar name used in her childhood had obviously left a lot unsaid.

She and Ned had known each other for two years—rather, two field seasons—and were good friends. She didn't want to make an issue out of the name change, so she let it pass. "It's not exhausting," she replied. "Remember, it's backfill, already excavated stuff, screened and all. It's not very hard packed."

Ned leaned the chair back against the desk and smiled. "Guess you don't have to be careful about excavation levels, either. You can just shovel the dirt without troweling it."

"Until I get to the plastic separating the backfill from the floor surface," she said. "Just under a meter to go. I'll have the floor exposed tomorrow."

Ned looked at her with a conspiratorial smile. "You still haven't explained why Greg gave you the okay to do this on your own. It's not ordinarily done, is it?"

Graciella returned the smile. "These aren't ordinary circumstances, Ned. This is my dissertation topic. My final season here. He was reluctant, though. Didn't want to start a precedent." The large site, Pot Creek Pueblo, was consistently used in a combination of field training and research. The Field Director for Archeology, Greg Parson, allowed individual projects at other sites on the 250 acres, and rarely at the Pot Creek site in isolated areas, but never where ongoing excavations were in progress. Continuity in data recording and field technique, as well as in training, demanded continuity in personnel. Greg was directly supervising excavation of this room block, Unit VII, and had been for three years. Graciella had been a graduate student on that unit two summers ago, but had been digging at a small, isolated pithouse site during this past summer.

"So what made him change policy?" Ned probed. "Did you go to Horace and Maria?"

"Absolutely not," Graciella said harshly. Maybe too harshly, she thought. She didn't want to overreact on this topic. She smiled, "That would never have worked, anyway. In fact, it would have cut me off permanently." Horace Stern, a linguist, was Director of the Center. By that title, he had general authority over the conduct of teaching and research at the Center, but individual project directors, whether teaching, research, or both, had primary control of their domains. Horace could technically override Greg on allocation of digging permission, but would never do so.

In Graciella's view, Horace was superb at low-keyed, hands-off management. She also knew that he was aggressively supportive of the Center's programs and faculty. Urging Stern to change Greg's policy would have permanently alienated her from her mentor and dissertation director.

"No," Graciella continued, "Greg gave me permission for a one-week test pit below the floor of Room 703. It was compensation for the change of excavation plans this summer." Graciella finished the beer, got up and went to the refrigerator. "Another beer?" she asked, taking one for herself.

Ned shook his head. "Why did he change plans?" Ned asked. "Wasn't he going to continue in that same block this summer, including what you're doing now?"

Graciella paused to open the bottle, then slowly returned to the bed. They were getting into a discussion area she wanted to avoid. She would have to be careful here. "Yeah," she said, deliberately not looking at Ned. "I was going to take 703 and 704 down subfloor. That's standard. But Greg also wanted to explore the area south of these rooms, into the ancient plaza. Either way, there's continuity and justification."

But the way it went, Graciella was locked out of Pot Creek this season and the subfloor excavation did not take place and Greg sent her across the acreage to work on a pithouse in hopes that her growing obsession about 703 would slacken. He had told no one of these nagging doubts about Graciella's motives and was, he had told her, protecting her from herself. It hadn't worked.

"So Greg decided to dig in the plaza this summer, and gave you permission to spend this week on Room 703?" Ned asked. "Sort of compensation for changing plans that originally involved you?"

Graciella rose and stretched. "Yeah, nice guy, right? I get to dig a week all by myself! A real holiday!" She inched toward the bathroom door. "Hey, I need a shower. See you at dinner, okay?"

"Okay." Ned opened the door. "I hope the rains don't shorten that week for you. Later." He shut the door as he left.

In the shower, Graciella let the hot water course over her shoulders and back, head down to feel the massaging effect on her neck. Did Ned know more than he allowed and was he probing for confirmation? Graciella didn't think so, and hadn't detected anything in his expression. He was certainly probing, though. Probably thinks there's something going on between us, Graciella thought, laughing to herself, while Greg just thinks I'm crazy. Which is worse for Ned and others to believe, truth or fiction, she wondered? For that matter, which is fiction?

The rain had stopped while she showered, and when she stepped out the sun had re-illuminated the landscape, sending bright light into the bathroom through the slanted shutters on the high window. The hachured pattern on the wall was reminiscent of the common motif on Taos Black-on-White pottery from the ancient pueblo. As she toweled her hair she caught her reflection in the medicine cabinet. Just a bit of sunburn on the nose and beneath the eyes, she noted. Used sun block, wore a hat, still can't escape it, she thought.

She gently pressed her cheekbones to test the redness. Her face was square above the cheeks, triangular below. The high-bridged nose and high cheekbones, and dark, almost almond shaped eyes hinted at Native American somewhere lost in her ancestry. She would have denied this, of course, two years ago. Now she wore her straight, black hair cropped at the shoulders and in bangs.

Although deep-set, the eyes always shone, and despite her twenty-three years, laugh wrinkles gave her a mirthful but older appearance. Her lower face was narrower, with a converging jaw line and almost pointed chin. Small, thin lips parenthesized with lines suggested the same laughter as the eyes; (she noted that grimacing, which she frequently did of late, would probably produce the same lines). Nevertheless, a happy demeanor often characterized her and, with her small frame (just under five feet, two inches and 102 pounds), had earned her an affection one often sees bestowed on little sisters.

There were times when she resented this, when she thought no one took her seriously. As she looked at her image, she wondered how seriously Horace and Ned and especially Greg took her commitment to this one-week project. She hadn't revealed the whole truth behind her almost compulsive attitude, and it may be that Greg was simply being indulgent.

She frequently conducted self-assessments at the mirror these past months. Not appraisals of the aging process, nor critiques of flawed beauty, for she burdened herself with none of the little conceits which a petite, attractive woman her age might have subconsciously justified. Rather, she viewed her physical image as a barometer to her inner self, and was increasingly careful of late to mask this. Does my expression reveal my thoughts? Does an apprehension show through? How transparently can I be read? Could Ned read my reluctance to discuss the dig today? She worried about telegraphing too much with a slightly turned mouth, subtle furrowing of the brow, or other outward indicator of an inward disposition.

Her anxiety about this had grown with the growing recognition that the chain of events over the past fourteen months had not been due to an overactive imagination, as Greg had initially suggested when she told him about the air in 703 the next day (and well he should have, she admitted at the time). Now, of course, the hour of truth was close approaching, and until then she wanted none of those close to her or the situation to have any reason to question either her professional motives or her personal stability. No one.

She moved out of the bathroom, slipped on a loose shift whose printed design had long since faded beyond recognition, and lay on the bed. "The hour of truth," she thought. What a dramatic phrase for so mundane an event: the removal of the final overburden to reveal the floor, basin, and center-posthole—the very same features she had revealed that first time, just over a year ago.

She closed her eyes. What would the truth _be_ at that hour? Were these past months simply journeys of the imagination? Would she discover only the prosaic below that floor? Or would she come full circle—another trite phrase—and re-enter that arcane world whose enigmatic messages had set her on this path of self-discovery to begin with?

Which did she want? The logical, practical conclusions of empirical science, returning her to the safety of a linear, predictable world she knew well? Or the uncertain reality of a past linked seamlessly with the future in a cyclical world, which could be as unsafe as it was unfamiliar?

She crossed into sleep with these contradictory worlds floating back and forth across the dull margin which precedes it. The alcohol and lack of food contributed to a fitful rest. In her dream she felt the coldness of the floor where the center-post had been, and began a cautious probing with her trowel. The fragments of the juniper post began to crumble into black and brittle cubes of charcoal, disappearing deeper in the posthole. Suddenly, charred kernels of maize filled the basin and they, too, began spilling into the hole and disappeared. Finally, the basin itself collapsed and Graciella fell through, but not with that interminable, slow motion fall so typical of nightmares. Instead, she fell quickly into a shallow ash pit and found herself in a kiva, its fire no longer bright, its glowing ashes radiating heat on her face and almost spectral shadows on the encircling wall.

Without awakening, Graciella drifted into deeper sleep as the fire's embers lost their last light. By first light of morning she would remember little of this, although the sunburned heat on her cheeks would require some attention.

While she and others in the compound slept, a faint light moved slowly up the mound of the excavation, stopping at Room 703. So faint it was that a casual onlooker would have been likely to miss noting it. But there were no onlookers. It moved furtively back and forth before coming to rest on the surface. The silence was penetrated by the brief call of a predatory owl. Then the soft *scritch* of a shovel's blade passing through loose earth, followed by the staccato *whump* of falling soil. *Scritch. Whump.* The muted sounds repeated into the night, unheard by all save the owl, which finally left its perch in frustration to seek prey in some quieter place.

3

Graciella awakened around five-thirty and tossed and dozed until a magpie announced dawn an hour later. She still felt some fatigue, and her face stung—she must have gotten more sun than she realized—but the adrenalin came quickly. Anticipation, she knew, of her second and (hopefully) decisive day at the site. She dressed, splashed cold water on her face, and applied sun block liberally but gingerly.

The walk to the dining hall along the lightly graveled nature trail took about six minutes as it followed the course of the creek, the Rio Grande del Rancho. The yellow-tan adobe of the dining hall loomed out of the surrounding forest without assaulting its harmony. Its curving walls accented the gentle contour of the terrace above the stream.

Graciella passed under the broad *portal* and entered. The vast dining room beyond the foyer was pierced by shafts of sunlight passing through the narrow twelve-foot-high eastern windows, illuminating tables, sage-green patterned carpet, and the white adobe wall opposite. The high overhead spotlights were off, and the expanse of adobe wall separating the two banks of windows left the rest of the interior darkened, giving the entire auditorium an austere appearance and setting for it a quiet mood.

She poured a cup of coffee and moved to a table in the darker portion. The cafeteria line would open at 7:00, about a minute from now. Three other early risers sat together at the back of the room, talking softly. The head count at the Center had decreased from over 100 a week ago to less than one dozen now, mostly graduate students in geology and archeology finishing individual projects and art students preparing their summer canvases for shipment back to their respective campuses. These students were all housed in *casitas* scattered in the forest at this southern end of the acreage.

The line opened and Graciella took a plate of scrambled eggs, hash-browns, and bacon. She was finishing her second cup of coffee when Ned came through the line and joined her. "Missed you at dinner last night," he said. "I knocked on your door once, but there was no answer."

"I took a long shower and then just crashed," Graciella said. "I guess I was more exhausted than I thought. Sorry."

"No matter. Better watch the sun today, though. Looks like it watched you a bit yesterday."

She touched her cheek. "It looks worse than it feels," she said. "After I get the rest of the fill out today I can partially cover the room. I'll be doing more troweling than shoveling at that point."

"When's Greg coming back?" Ned asked. Greg had completed his preliminary report and taken it back to Southern Methodist University in Dallas, but was returning to check on Graciella and other student projects just before fall classes began.

"Tomorrow or the next day," she answered. "Horace should hear from him today." She looked around. A few others had come in, but Horace and Maria had not. They usually came for breakfast coffee, but not before seven-thirty.

Graciella checked the wall clock. Seven-twenty. "Got to go," she said, rising. She gathered her plate, cup and silverware on her breakfast tray.

"Mind if I come out later on?" Ned asked. "I'd like to see the room."

She pursed her lips and frowned slightly. "Why don't you wait a bit," she said. "I don't know how long this will take, but I probably won't go below floor until tomorrow. You can see it for sure in the morning." Using "probably" made it not quite a big lie, she hoped. This was both a scientific and a personal thing, today, and the personal thing had to be private.

"Fair enough," he said. "Good luck."

She returned her tray and made two sandwiches for lunch. She walked back to the fort, filled her canteen, grabbed her red-banded straw hat, lunch bag, and field pack, and drove across the highway to the site.

The rain had been brief enough not to create muddy ruts in the road, although flatter places had standing water and the area next to the site on the south was mucky. She pulled up to the drier slope of the rising mounds and parked.

The site covered just over eight acres and consisted of nine buried room blocks. Seven of these had been at least partially excavated over the past forty years, and most had revealed contiguous units of rectangular rooms, originally terraced in two to three stories in their central parts, with associated court-yards and circular subterranean kivas.

Pot Creek Pueblo was not as impressive as the magnificent Chaco Canyon complex. Chaco was sprawling, filled with high drama in its masonry architecture and cosmological connections and extensive causeways: the Mecca of the Southwest. At Pot Creek the small population was aggregated through time into nine apartment buildings made not of stone but of coursed adobe. No highways announced its presence to the outside world and pilgrims never drew themselves towards it. Nor was Pot Creek Pueblo as colorfully located as the beautiful Bandelier National Monument, with its inverted ecosystem, closer to Santa Fe.

In some ways, though, it had an archeological significance more unique that these popular tourist destinations. The source and sudden disappearance of the Chacoan peoples and those at Bandelier remained largely an unsolved mystery, while the Pot Creek peoples not only had an origin that was rather carefully dated and sourced, their living descendants were by now well-identified as the peoples of Picuris and Taos.

Most of the excavated units at Pot Creek had been backfilled after excavation to protect the structures for possible future re-excavation. Hence, both previously- and yet-to-be-excavated units alike appeared as mounds supporting a thick cover of sagebrush and *chamisa*. Most rose fifteen or more feet above the surrounding terrain. The top of Graciella's room block, Unit VII, could not be seen until she reached the top of the nearer Unit VI. The two units were separated by a broad plaza area only partially excavated, and a kiva as yet untouched.

From the distance of Unit VI, it appeared to Graciella that the plastic covering had held. Good. The opening would be reasonably dry. She reached the top of Unit VII and put down her field kit, lunch and canteen. The sun was already suspended brightly in a cloudless sky.

Something, however, was not right. Almost immediately it struck her. Her backdirt! Where was it? At least six cubic yards of backdirt from yester-day's seven hours of excavation were—how was it possible?—gone!

Frantically, she kicked and shoved away the rocks holding the upper perimeter of the black plastic, then threw open the cover, forcefully willing it to expose a gaping meter-deep excavation. "No!" she yelled. "No! NO!" She fell to her knees and clutched at the fresh dirt that now filled her excavation to the surface of yesterday morning. "No! Christ!" she choked back a sob, then rocked back on her heels and stared incredulously at the evenly filled square, and then at the freshly-scraped surface next to it where her backdirt had been.

Slowly, Graciella stood. "Who did this?" she asked aloud. "Who would do it?" Then, "why?" Softer, again, "why?" She looked around. A whisper now: "why?" Slowly, she collected her thoughts and focused on the scene before her. Now, really, she thought, who would want to do this? She surely had no enemies, had she? Could any other grad students be upset that she had received permission for this dig? None. Most had already returned to school; the few remaining had their own projects.

Perhaps it was a practical joke! But who? Ned? Not likely. Even those she knew who occasionally played practical jokes—and every dig experiences some; it was an acceptable means of removing social stratification and maintaining camaraderie amid tension—even they would not stoop to cruelty. This was cruel! This cost her one day out of the seven precious days she had! The realization removed her dismay and replaced it with anger. She would find out who did this and make them undo it! By God, they would pay!

"Now, calm down," she told herself. "Let's think this through." She paced slowly over the top of the mound. There should be footprints, she thought. She left yesterday as the rains had begun to sieve through the sky. That was about 3:15. The rains came heavy after that until. . .when? She was out of the shower and the sun was bright. What time was it? Probably just before five. Maybe as early as 4:30? Whoever did this must have come over here after the rain, between 4:30 and nightfall, around 8:30 on a clear night.

After the rain! There should be tracks! Had she seen any driving in? She couldn't remember. On the mound here? She moved carefully, inspecting the surface. The culprit almost had to have come the same way, over a narrow and dusty trail made muddy by the rain. She backtracked her route, down Unit VII, up and over Unit VI, then down to the Explorer. Not any recognizable tracks other than her own this morning! She walked along the road, looking intently at the still muddy areas. In places there were obviously two sets of tire tracks!

She knelt down and examined them carefully. Damn! They all looked identical. She walked alternate routes back to Unit VII. Not a trace of any-thing. She folded the plastic and lay stones on it. She picked up her field pack, canteen, and lunch and stood for a moment looking. Am I missing anything? My shovel! Did the criminal add insult by actually using her shovel to refill her excavation? But the bastard wouldn't know her shovel was left here, and would have come prepared.

Chances are, she thought, my shovel is where I left it. Under 1.2 meters of twice-excavated fill! "Damn you!" she shouted from the mound top. She was answered by the trill of a hummingbird, pausing briefly to inspect the red band of her hat, then darting up and away. The doppler effect of the falling pitch of its whistle sounded almost sinister. She turned and went back down towards her Explorer. She tossed her gear in and looked once more at the tracks, the mud, and her tires. Two sets of prints. Identical. Then it struck her: of course they are identical; they're both from the Explorer! Yesterday, she sat here in the rain for some time, leaving one set as she left. The second set she had made just now.

She drove back disconsolate but determined. "By God," she muttered between clenched teeth, "no one will stop me!" There are only two things to do, now, she reasoned. One is to find the person who did it, and the other is to make up for my lost time. She had formulated a plan to achieve both by the time she returned to her quarters.

It was now 8:15. Ned would be in his lab, and Horace Stern would either be in quarters or in the Director's Office at the fort. The restored compound was in a layout typical of most western forts. Graciella's apartment was in the Officers Quarters at the western perimeter. This structure lay broadside to the parade grounds on the east, at the far end of which was the main fort building. Bordering the parade grounds on the north were an additional billet for an officer, now transformed into the geology lab where Ned worked, and the Commander's Quarters, a two-bedroom house occupied appropriately by the Director.

Along the south side was the dispensary and surgeon's quarters, housing archeological laboratories. Next to this structure was a supply depot used now for processing, cataloging and curation of artifacts. It also housed excavation supplies and equipment.

It was to this building that Graciella first went. The storage section had its own exterior door. It was locked. Graciella opened it with her key and turned on the light. The roughly square twenty-by-twenty foot room had slotted steel shelving along two walls and an island of shelves in the center. On either side of the doorway wall were cabinets. Along the remaining wall were shovels, mattocks, hoes, screens for screening backdirt, and wheelbarrows.

Graciella went immediately to the shovels and began examining them carefully. The blade of each shovel glistened. After each season, all large iron tools were thoroughly cleaned and coated with a film of boiled linseed oil. She touched each blade. All had the coating, but none was fresher than several days: tacky to the touch but not wet. She went to the file cabinet and pulled the inventory folder. There were her initials for the shovel she had checked out. Those remaining on the inventory were all present, sealed, and ready for next season. Whoever had done it had used no shovel from this supply.

She leafed through the other inventory folders. There were several pieces of equipment still checked out, she noticed. Daniel Sheffield had a 30-meter tape and a Brunton compass. He was still conducting the archeological survey of sites in nearby Miranda Canyon. Wouldn't need a shovel for that. Andrea "Andy" Abbott had a tape and a transit with stadia rod. Andy was working with the New Mexico State Archaeologist on a survey and salvage project near Peñasco, where a highway was being widened. They had their own shovels plus a crew to wield them. Andy was doing the mapping. No one else had equipment checked out.

Graciella locked the door as she left. There was one other source of shovels at Ft. Burgwin: the maintenance crew. The Facilities Manager, Felix Mondragon, generally ran a crew of three to four people during the summer. Two were still here. They kept the area mowed, replaced and graded gravel on the roads, picked up garbage for the Center's landfill daily, and did whatever else Felix told them to do. Shovels were used frequently. There were several places shovels might be kept. There was a small tool room on the corner of the east courtyard of the fort building, near the Director's office. There was a larger storage room at the opposite corner of the same courtyard. Then there were the trucks used by the maintenance crew and manager: they frequently left tools in truck beds. Inventory was probably not very faithfully kept, thought Graciella. She didn't have keys to either storeroom, although she could ask Stern or Felix to let her in. Occasionally, however, both rooms were left open during the day, since keys were never given to the workmen.

She hesitated before entering the eastern courtyard. If Stern saw her snooping around, he'd ask questions. Well, so what, she thought. She was certainly going to tell him what happened; after all, this was a violation of ethical conduct at least! She would prefer to tell him after discovering who did it, of course, and decided to snoop at the risk of confrontation. Whatever happens, she thought, I can't waste time.

The large tool storeroom was open, and Stern was not in his office. His administrative assistant, Karen Brown, was on the phone in the outer office, but would probably take no account of Graciella even if she did see her. No one was in storeroom and the light was off. Graciella entered and switched on the light. The place was fairly chaotic, but six to eight shovels, short and long handled, square and round bladed, lay against one wall. She began running her hand over and behind the blade of each, to identify any fresh earth. A few did indeed have dirt and clay, all dried and heavily caked on. It was difficult to tell how recently they had been used. Could she tell by the color? Perhaps if she took a shovel to the doorway for better light.

A large shadow suddenly darkened the doorway just as she turned. Graciella jumped and the shovel clattered noisily to the floor. "Is there something you need, Miss Graciella?" asked the shadow.

"Felix! You startled me!" she exclaimed. He was over six feet, slender in the hips, but barrel-chested. Graciella figured he was probably in his forties. His wife lived with him in the manager's house just south of the Fort complex. They had no children.

She decided to learn what she could without telling much, but to tell more if she thought she could learn more. "I just wondered, Felix, are these all of your shovels or do you keep some elsewhere?" She wished she could read the expression on his face better, but he faced her from the bright open doorway, which he continued to block.

"Elsewhere, Miss Graciella?" asked Felix. She was positive his expression was skeptical. "Yes, we keep a shovel in each pickup. Do you need one?"

Graciella realized she was not good at this. She'd better tell him. "No, Felix," she said. "Last evening, someone took a shovel over to Pot Creek and filled up my room with dirt from the excavation." She picked up the shovel she had dropped. "All of our archeology shovels are clean and stored away. I was trying to find out if someone could have used one of these shovels."

Felix frowned. "One of _my_ shovels? My men? You think maybe me?"

"Oh, no, Felix!" Graciella reached out and touched his arm. "Not you or your men! Certainly not! I just wondered, since I found the room open, if maybe someone could have taken one, or maybe one out of a pickup." She smiled weakly. "I don't know where else someone would get a shovel."

"You know who it might have been?" Felix asked. "One of the students, playing a trick?"

"I don't know. I can't imagine. But now all my work yesterday I must do over! And if I can't find out who did it, it might happen again. I have only this week to dig!" Graciella caught herself and took a deep breath. She was rapidly becoming emotional and did not want Felix to sense any hysteria.

"Let me tell you, Miss Graciella, about my men," Felix said in a tone that suggested an important lesson would follow. "They are simple but good men. They work hard, real _trabajaderos_. They fear God. They know that at Pot Creek, you dig up the _Teotles_—the ancient people. They see where you keep some of the skulls. They sometimes ask, where do you keep their souls?" Felix's eyes narrowed and he came a step closer. "They are superstitious men, Miss Graciella, and they know that at Pot Creek you have released witches. They would never go there alone. They would never touch the _Tlal-tepetl_—the mounds—with a shovel!" He stood straight and smiled at her. "Of course, I am not superstitious and am not afraid of pueblo witches. I also do not like to fill holes with dirt, unless I was the one who made the hole."

Graciella handed Felix the shovel as he stepped aside. "Thank you, Felix. I know it wasn't you or your men. Please forget I mentioned it." She walked out of the storeroom.

"Miss Graciella," Felix called. She stopped and turned. "I keep this room locked when I am not close by. But I will check. I will also check the pickups."

"Thank you very much, Felix."

As Graciella left, heading for the Director's Office and Horace Stern, she failed to notice the figure listening intently just inside the doorway of the office not fifteen feet from the storeroom. The room was used for photocopying and long distance phoning by faculty and staff. The light inside was off, and as Graciella passed by it, the door furtively closed.

4

Horace Stern was a large man. Squarely built at six feet and 215 pounds, he was not fat. His collar-length hair was salt-and-pepper, on its way to the white of his goatee. Square jaw, blue eyes under bushy eyebrows the color of his hair; his vitality and muscularity suggested a man younger than his fifty-nine years. His appearance also suggested a sturdy Scandinavian stock, but his was second generation Swiss.

With a PhD from Berkeley and a long career at Arizona, Horace had worked the various Tanoan languages of the Rio Grande pueblos for over thirty years. His sociolinguistic work with the Taos and Picuris dialects of Tiwa had attracted him to Ft. Burgwin while George Trager was working there in the late '60s, and in turn this association had led to his transfer to Southern Methodist University, which owned the Center, two years ago. Gruff on the exterior and completely impatient with shallow intellects or shoddy research, he was a loyal and accommodating friend to those who displayed energy and competence. He also played the violin with professional skill and devotion, which endeared him to the arts in Taos and at the Center. He had been appointed Director last year, an appointment widely supported by both science and the arts.

Horace's gruff exterior was balanced by his wife, Maria, whose manner was warm and outgoing. Twelve years his junior, Maria had met Horace when she was working at the clinic at Taos Pueblo, where she still volunteered. Then Maria Ramos, she had earned a nursing degree at the University of New Mexico in Albuquerque. After working in frustration in numerous clinics and encountering the rigid incompatibility between the Western medical model and traditional medical practice, she studied ethnology in the UNM Anthropology Department while working off-season at the Taos Pueblo and other Indian Health Service Clinics. At these she had observed some of the ritual indigenous to native medicine, and much of the skepticism with which non-Indians viewed such practices. Maria had hopes of bringing together the native and the Western, but knew enough of the former to recognize critical areas of incompatibility.

She had a perfectly oval face framed exactly by center-parted black hair that fell over her shoulders. Her diminutive narrow nose separated wide, large black eyes with long eyelashes. The eyes now flashed as she and Horace engaged in lively discussion. "No, I don't think it was wise to give her permission," said Maria. "You should have waited."

Horace shifted his frame on the couch in their quarters, took a slow sip from his iced tea, and gave her a benign smile. "Now, my dear, calm yourself," he said in a voice that was proxy for an affectionate pat on the behind. "I know Graciella well and find her to be quite capable. You fret too much."

"Don't patronize, husband," Maria jabbed in staccato notes, while her thin, pouting lips softened these with a challenge of humor. She and Horace had long enjoyed the parry-and-thrust verbal engagements of a couple who not only complemented each other, but refracted each other's personalities while dueling. "I don't doubt her capability; I merely question your discretion," Maria said, sitting at the small table opposite him. "Greg holds command in that arena. You should have let him call the shots. He arrives tomorrow, as I believe you told her?"

"Tomorrow," Horace replied, "as I believe you understand, is the third day of a seven-day marathon for our young colleague. Would you shorten still further her time in deference to some sense of protocol?" Horace gestured with his glass for more tea. The pitcher was at her elbow on the table. She poured slowly, with deliberation, then poured a glass for herself. Graciella had spent the last twenty minutes with them in the Commander's Quarters, not finding Horace in the office. She had explained directly what had happened, or rather what she had found, at the site this morning. She claimed not to know who might have done the deed. No, she had not yet talked to Ned nor to the graduate students still around. Yes, she planned to. But her immediate concern was her schedule. Did Horace know when Greg was to arrive?

Upon hearing that he was to arrive the next day, Graciella had explained the need for more drastic action. Greg, after all, was coming to check on her progress. As of now, that progress was zero. She needed to have the floor exposed when Greg arrived. Would Horace give her permission to use the backhoe?

"Well, you should have called Greg, at least, before giving permission," Maria said. She was serious now; no more jousting. "Even if only out of courtesy."

Horace and Greg were good colleagues, though not close friends, and they absolutely agreed on turf authority and responsibility. Maria was sure that, positions reversed, Greg would have called Horace.

"Look, my love," Horace reverted now to his term of affection, "Greg is busy. He's writing a syllabus. He's editing his final report. And he's preparing to return here tomorrow. I don't think he needs to be bothered with a minor request. You wait. He will agree with my decision." He got up, walked to Maria, bent down and kissed her forehead. "He'll be happy to have an excavation ready for inspection! I, on the other hand, would go dancing naked on the parade ground if I knew all my problems would be so readily resolved."

Maria lifted her chin, as if inspecting Horace through bifocals. "Spare the gods that indelicate moment, White man," she sniffed. "For surely afterwards the land would yield dust."

He waved her comment off. "To the office, my dear. I've work to get done." He left through the kitchen, heading into the parade ground towards the fort. Maria followed him to the door. She stood there awhile, looking across the complex, thinking about Pot Creek and wondering who the enemy was.

◇◇◇

Graciella sat under the juniper at the southern edge of the site, eating the lunch she had made at breakfast. She looked again at her watch. It was 11:00 a.m. Felix should be here with the backhoe by 11:30, she thought. She was relieved the discussion with Stern had gone so well. She had emphasized the importance of using the backhoe to recover her lost time.

Stern had asked only how secure she was in operating the backhoe and the accessibility of that part of the mound. She had reassured him on both points. She had used both the hoe and front loader the past two seasons, and was comfortable with the equipment. Stern initially had wanted Felix to operate it, but Graciella had explained how delicate the task was in avoiding walls and floor. She had done this before; knew how to fine-tune the large shovel's movements. In the end, Stern had given the okay with the provision that Felix or someone be there with her. Fair enough, she thought.

Maria had remained quiet during the discussion, but Graciella had the impression that she was against the decision. Perhaps she was fearful that it was unsafe. Graciella smiled at the thought. The unsafe part might come afterward, with the troweling. Graciella's attention was drawn to the sound of a heavy diesel engine: the backhoe was on its way. She looked at her watch. Eleven thirty-five. She got up to meet Felix.

As much as Felix had protested any feeling of superstition regarding the site, Graciella noticed that he kept his distance as she positioned the backhoe. The machine was almost an antique: a forty-five year old Case-320 industrial tractor, with a backhoe and front-end loader. She drove forward to the top of the mound, then worked the tractor around backwards, judging the distance she would need for the extended backhoe arm.

Satisfied, she tilted the blade of the front shovel and lowered it, digging it into the surface and raising the front of the tractor off its wheels. She reversed the seat and sat, facing back, at the controls of the backhoe. She lowered the pneumatic stabilizers until the rear wheels were suspended, checked the shovel movement on the hoe, and carefully lowered the arm towards the center of the backfilled square that was her target. At this point, Felix appeared at her right side. "You gonna be able to see what you're doing?" he yelled over the sound of the engine.

"No problem," she yelled back. She had done this kind of thing before.

"How you gonna to know when you're deep enough?" he asked.

"When I bring up my shovel in the backhoe," she yelled back. Felix retreated as she made the first cut. The fill dirt was very soft and it fell easily away from the harder, drier adobe walls of the room. This made it relatively easy to excavate by placing the hoe just inside the walls.

In less than ten minutes, she had extricated the shovel, motioning to Felix to recover it from the dirt pile. She made four more careful grabs with the hoe, then idled it and climbed down. She took the shovel with her and consolidated some of the remaining fill in the excavation. Her trowel indicated that she was now an average of about 30 cm. from the floor. She climbed back up, scooped and emptied the consolidated fill, and secured the hoe. She then reversed the seat, released the supports, and took the backhoe off the mound.

"It's all yours, Felix," she yelled, stepping down. "*Muchisimo gracias, amigo.*"

Felix approached the idling backhoe. "Miss Graciella," he said, "please do not continue with this alone. It is not safe for you to be here."

"I'll be fine, Felix," she replied.

He frowned at her. "Then be careful." He paused as he climbed onto the tractor. "By the way, I checked all the shovels. They're all there and no one has used them."

"Thanks, Felix." She waved as he engaged the gears and drove off.

Graciella spent the next three hours with shovel and trowel in Room 703. By three-twenty it was cleared except for the center basin. She now hesitated, looking at the 2-3 cm of fill covering the basin. Will this happen again, she wondered?

It did not. By three-forty the room and basin were clean, as they had been left two years ago. She ran her hand over the basin and its post-hole. There was no detectable air and no change in temperature. She stood and surveyed the room. And then it struck her: it had changed! From her perspective, standing against the southwest wall, it was obvious. The slump to the northeast was now dramatic! It was much greater than it had been in the original excavation. She needed her field records from that season. She would redraw the profile and compare.

"Hi, Grace. Can I see your monument to archeological technique?" Ned's smiling face appeared as he ascended the mound. "You said I should wait, but I'll be out tomorrow checking maps."

"Come ahead," Graciella said. She pointed out the center post, burned areas on the walls, and the slump in the structure.

"So this indicates a kiva below the room?" Ned asked.

"Yes. Or at least some rather deep feature," Graciella said. "An earlier room or plaza surface below this would not allow such a tilt in the floor and walls as you see."

"Fascinating. Are you going to go subfloor now?"

"Yes, but first I need to profile the angle of this floor. It's changed a bit." Graciella paused, frowning. "Ned," she changed her tone. "I'm staying here tonight. I'm not coming to dinner."

"For heaven's sake, Grace," Ned said. "You don't expect a repeat of yesterday!" Graciella had told him of last night's incident after she had arranged for the backhoe with Felix, earlier.

"I'm taking no chances, Ned. Can you wait here a minute while I drive back for my bed-roll?"

Ned bowed deeply. "I'll do better than that, milady," he said. "I'll fetch it for you after dinner and bring you something to eat."

"Thank you, Ned," Graciella smiled. "I just can't afford any other set-backs. Greg's coming in tomorrow."

"No problem," said Ned. "I take it you still have no list of suspects?"

"None," she replied, "unless I put everyone on it!"

"Even me?" asked Ned in mock incredulity.

"Even myself!" laughed Graciella. "Maybe I sleepwalk and have a death wish."

◇◇◇

When Ned left, she profiled the east wall on grid paper she had in her field kit. It sloped down toward the north by just over 20 degrees. She would swear it had not been more than 10 degrees originally. This really was inexplicable! The centuries since abandonment had led to a 10-degree slope as the underlying fill of the kiva settled and weathered from seeping moisture. Now, in the space of just over 12 months, it had slumped another 10 degrees! How? Nothing had changed here. Subsequent excavations had been on the opposite side of the mound. What could have disturbed the underlying fill? How did it become destabilized? Nothing had changed.

Nothing, she thought, except the strange events that began with that coolness from 703 on a hot June afternoon, and perhaps had not yet ended. It was now 4:15, and she heard thunder in the distance. Rain would again visit the ancient site. God, it was going to be a long vigil before dawn. Her attention was drawn to a hawk circling above, searching for moving prey. An omen? She dismissed the thought and walked back to her Explorer to record her field notes. She finished by 4:45. She closed her field pack and stepped outside, raising her canteen for a drink. She glanced upward. It appeared that the rains might pass to the south.

The hawk had narrowed its spiral and was closer. Then she realized that it was not the noble hunter after all, but a scavenger. The hawk was, instead, a vulture. And the prey it sought would not be moving. She shuddered only slightly, for she was not in the least superstitious.

5

Dr. Gregory Parson eased the rented Pontiac Firebird off Interstate 25 at exit 282 in Santa Fe, on the final leg of his destination. He had taken the 8:10 a.m. Southwestern flight from Dallas to Albuquerque, then rented the car for the 2-1/2 hour drive to the research center. The sun was already baking the hills. From Santa Fe he would leave the arid and dissected table land where the Rocky Mountains made their southernmost statement on the landscape. He would shortly enter the valley where the Rio Grande had incised its deep pathway along a violent course now favored by white-water enthusiasts.

It was a welcome change of scenery. He appreciated the stark beauty of the desert southwest—his early fieldwork had been done on the Mogollon Rim in southern New Mexico—but the sculptured relief of the northern mountains always exhilarated him. Especially in August. He adjusted the air conditioner to push more air. He passed the Santa Fe Opera, perched high to his left, and began the descent into the colorful valley of Tesuque Pueblo and Pojoaque.

At 32, Greg was as content as he had ever hoped to be. Hired by SMU with a fresh doctorate from Arizona State five years ago, he had worked in southwest archeology since adolescence, volunteering first and then receiving professional training. He had spent two seasons at Black Mesa and had run his own small dig in the Gila National Forest out of Silver City.

Tall and slender, with sandy hair and a ruddy complexion, Greg was easygoing but intense. Unmarried, his only passions were research and writing. His single-minded focus made him the appropriate model of the absent-minded professor, as he frequently forgot or ignored minor items of occasional importance such as belts or color-coordinated clothing.

His position afforded him the opportunity to teach and conduct research simultaneously—in the field at Taos and in the classroom and laboratory at SMU's main campus in Dallas. His students, undergraduates included, often acquired the same intensity, and occasionally the same sense of personal style. Their training, however, was superb. Greg rewarded commitment with favored research projects and personal guidance, and his graduate students typically completed their dissertations in less time than others in the department.

Grace had been one of those to receive Greg's professional blessing. Now in her third summer as a graduate student, she needed one more field season to complete her research. She had been bright and energetic from the beginning, quick to make insightful connections from the archeological record. She had expressed an early interest in the challenge of distinguishing between the pithouse as a structure for habitation and its later development into a kiva as a structure for sacred ritual. The challenge gave her opportunity to seek answers from ethnohistory as well as archeology, for these circular underground structures were ubiquitous in the pueblo southwest.

This appealed very much to Greg. Working from the past forward and from the present backward, converging on a complex social-structural problem, combining different but complementary methodologies, using analogy in a rigorous hypothetico-deductive approach, this all had a refined elegance that was of compelling interest to a disciplined mind.

So he had supported Grace's interest after her first season. As a TA, she had been assigned supervision of the two rooms most likely to overlie a kiva and, when this was partially confirmed by the slump of the floor in Room 703, Greg had planned for her to continue this season. These plans had changed, however, and she was given a pithouse site instead—still within her research trajectory, he knew, since she had expected and acknowledged the need for further experience in the broad variations of pithouse architecture. To help hasten her research, he had offered to let her stay on after the current season to go subfloor in 703 and identify the features below.

No, he reflected, this was not entirely true. She could not possibly, alone, get far into the kiva in a single week! He also figured that in her compulsive need, she was blinded to this realization—or did it simply not matter to her? Greg massaged the thought for a moment: probably it didn't matter. Getting below the floor was infinitely more important than what might happen afterwards, he knew. The floor with its basin and center-post had been her personal albatross for two seasons now. And that was why he had given her this week. It was also why he had re-assigned her responsibilities this season—over her uncharacteristic objections—thus keeping her from confronting this obsession during the busy field school. Better to have this concluded in isolation.

It had begun with that strange experience Grace had told him about, in the floor of Room 703, season before last. They had agreed that it had been her imagination. He had thought she had dismissed it, but she had refused to let it go. A month or so later, Grace had insisted on returning to the room this season, and back at SMU during the year she had been moody and unusually pensive. Crazy, he thought, that something so trivial had grown to overwhelming importance. In her mind.

He slowed as he approached the first stoplight in Española. The digital temperature on the revolving bank sign indicated 97 degrees, and he touched the temperature control to see if it was at its coldest setting. It was. Beyond Española and the long stretch that included San Juan Pueblo, he would climb into a cooler world. He glanced at the digital clock. Ten forty-six. He should be there by noon.

She should be through the floor by now. He wanted her to be over this. There was too much he didn't understand. We all have our personal demons, Greg said to himself. But most had some logical cause: an unhappy childhood, an abusive love affair, a catastrophic personal failure. Grace had none of these. Most demons don't suddenly emerge. Hers appeared without warning. So Grace had become Graciella. Okay, he could live with that. But with it came a subtle personality change. Her attention would frequently wander. She would daydream. Greg could accept the eccentricity of changing her name, but he couldn't face losing her brilliant mind to an unknown adversary with an obviously powerful influence. So he relented on her need to excavate this kiva.

Greg recalled her acute disappointment when he announced, in early spring, that the field school would not be excavating subfloor this season. He had explained that it was more important to identify the room block perimeter first, and to do this meant moving to the contiguous rooms east and south of the excavated rooms.

"We find the perimeter, identify the plaza surface," he had patiently said. "From this we know the architectural context of what we have. It gives us better horizontal control." She had nodded assent, but was obviously numbed with disappointment. He had tried to explain, further, the logic of using adjacent plaza surfaces as a stratigraphic control. "If we go sub-surface in the plaza, we're getting a cleaner picture of occupation sequence, Grace; we can tie earlier features below the rooms to earlier plaza levels with less ambiguity."

He remembered, even now, his words and the incongruous expression on Grace's face. She really hadn't been keyed to the scientific logic of his explanation, he recalled. Of course not, an inner voice told him; her motivation has shifted to some other, or inner, domain. And that, Greg now admitted, was a third and non-scientific reason for his decision to change excavation plans this past season. Give her time to get over the obsession, he had told himself, give her a season at a pithouse, and she'll forget this business. But she hadn't forgotten. Each week this season she had begged to finish 703. He had finally acquiesced. He would give her one week, after the close of the field school, to conduct a subfloor excavation. But, he insisted, it had to be done with the same methodical patience, the same technical skill, the same careful controls, and the same data collection regimen they had always used.

"Of course!" she had responded without hesitation, and had literally straightened up and brightened as if a depressing burden had been lifted from her small frame. Indeed, it probably had.

Now he was on his way to see whether his judgment, and her sanity, was sound. She would be through the floor and she would find there an end to her apprehension. And she would return, under his guidance, to the science he knew and understood so well. She must!

He was into the mountain bottleneck, now, just past the old Embudo Station, where the narrow-gauge track had reached Taos and beyond until World War II. It was cooler outside, while the air conditioner was blasting chilled air inside. And Greg was perspiring.

◇◇◇

The night had passed uneventfully. There had been only a light rain. Ned had brought her bed roll, some hot enchiladas, and a cold beer. They had sat talking until just after dusk, and Ned had left. There fell only a light rain. Graciella had spread her sleeping bag in the open back of the Explorer, read awhile by the light of a Coleman lantern, and finally—at 10 o'clock—extinguished it and fell asleep.

She awakened at dawn, quickly climbed up to the excavation, and confirmed with relief that it had been undisturbed. It was six-thirty. She drove back to the Officers' Quarters, took a quick shower, and had a bowl of cereal. She was back at the site within the hour.

Graciella checked the string against the east wall with her line level. She had left it in place after profiling the wall yesterday. It was off horizontal, and she moved the north end upward until the line was plumb and marked the spot. Two inches lower. The floor and wall had tilted another two degrees or so overnight! Unexcavated fill atop the adjacent north wall had also slumped, spilling some into the room. This is frightening, Graciella thought. The under-lying debris of six centuries had to be stable and solid, not loose. She stood in silence, her will competing with what her eyes held before her. Her rational mind urged a delay until Greg arrived, just to be safe. Her emotional mind pressed her to move forward with the excavation. Will it be safe for me to dig below floor level? she asked herself. The answer was so close, after so many months. She swallowed, and the taste in her mouth was not fear.

She had to try. She had brought a small one-hand mattock—a short handled digging tool with adze-like blade projecting one way and pointed pick projecting the other—and would use the pick end to cut through the packed adobe floor. She chose the area between the curbed basin and the east wall. She used the pick to inscribe a half-meter square on the floor, where she would begin her sub-floor excavation. She then struck a hard blow midway between basin and wall.

Three things happened simultaneously, and so rapidly that Graciella had no time to react. A high-pitched scream that combined with the sound of escaping air, not unlike a whistling teakettle, pierced the silence. Fragments of desiccated wood from the center-post to her left, together with crumbled debris, were blown a meter or more upward by a surge of cool air. The floor below her sank and tilted precipitously, causing her to lose balance and roll down into the sinking north wall.

She gasped and choked on the swirling dust amid the falling debris, trying to claw her way up the still slipping floor surface. Through the partially subsiding cloud of dust she saw the north wall, against which her lower body still lay, begin to move towards her. My God, she thought, the wall is collaps-ing. I'm going to be buried!

She slid further downward as the floor continued its tilt and turned her more vertically. The advancing wall closed upon her and she threw her arms across her face in reflex as another scream, this one definitely human, rose above the debris and the mound, its wail careening against the surrounding hills.

Her last thought before losing consciousness was the curious realization that the scream had not been hers. Then all was quiet, cold, dark.

6

Holy Cross Hospital in Taos was an unassuming adobe structure back then, single story, with vigas extended from its upper walls in the traditional Spanish Colonial pattern. Its soft, unbroken curves and its rich earth color gave it the appearance of a well-kept 19th Century hacienda. Only the windsock and adjacent care-flight helipad betrayed its more modern and somber use, while the cross beside its entry stood as a reminder that healing involves more than the pills and procedures of Western medicine.

Inside, it is sanitized and clean and has the same disinfectant smell of any clinic or hospital where illness is treated and health is sometimes restored. Here, in room 14, semi-private, Graciella awoke at 2:30 p.m. Completely disoriented, dazed from a throbbing pain in her head, she blinked her eyes and moaned.

Lying on her side, her focus revealed an elderly Hispanic man sitting beside the adjacent bed. In the bed lay a woman, an IV line running from her right wrist to a plastic liquid-filled bag hanging above. The old man held her hand.

Graciella blinked again. Where was she? Her head was pounding so! She closed her eyes, tried to think, but thinking seemed to intensify the throbbing. I'm in some hospital, she reasoned. Why? She strained to recall. At least she knew who she was. Think, she commanded, what was I doing last? What can I remember?

She slowly visualized the Explorer. . .my Explorer, she thought. Near sagebrush and juniper. The site! I was excavating? No. Room was clean, undisturbed. Tilted.

The picture began to congeal. Oh, God. The pick in her hand. The rush of ancient air. Tilting. . .falling. . .the scream. "Oh, God!" Graciella moaned aloud. The old man looked at her in alarm. Then a hand touched her right shoulder. She turned her head.

"That's all right, Miss," said the figure in white. "You're safe here." A short Indian girl in a nurse's uniform stood beside her, smiling and patting her shoulder comfortingly. Her name tag read *A. Lujan.* "You had a nasty fall, but you're going to be okay."

"Where is this?" asked Graciella.

"You're in Holy Cross Hospital," Nurse Lujan answered. "You've been sleeping. Can you remember what happened?"

Graciella brought her hand to her right temple. A bandage covered it. There was gauze on her left wrist and right elbow, she noticed. "Yes," she replied. "I was excavating a room. It began to sink. It caved in on me." She looked anxiously at the nurse. "How bad am I hurt?" she asked.

"No broken bones," said Nurse Lujan. "A few cuts and scratches. And you have a slight concussion." She lowered her voice and stared deeply into Graciella's eyes. "Maybe you should have been more careful."

"What. . .?" Graciella blinked, trying to will the headache away. "No, I. . .this should not have happened. The room should not have collapsed."

Nurse Lujan frowned. "Maybe you were in the wrong place," she said. Her tone seemed somehow a warning, slicing through professional dispassion. "Many things happen that shouldn't if we are where we should not be." She gave Graciella a piercing look. "Do not work alone."

"What. . .what do you mean?"

Nurse Lujan backed away. "You rest now," she said. "The doctor will be in shortly." She left before Graciella could ask who had brought her in.

Graciella drifted into a restless sleep punctuated by her headache. When she awakened next, the old man had gone and Greg Parson and Maria Stern stood on either side of her. Both smiled at her as she opened her eyes. "Oh," Graciella whispered. "How long have you been here?"

"Not long," said Greg. "How are you feeling?"

"My head is splitting," Graciella answered. "Can someone get me some aspirin?"

Maria put her hand on the side rail. "I'm sorry, Graciella," she said. "They won't give you any pain killers for awhile. You have a slight concussion." Maria turned on the reading light above the bed. "Let me see your eyes."

Graciella looked up at her. "Are they okay?" she asked.

Maria patted her arm. "They look fine. No dilation." She stood up. "I know you hurt, but you look so much better than when I brought you in," she said.

"You!" Graciella said. "You found me?"

"Maria's been here the whole time," Greg smiled at Maria. "Thank God you're okay. When I arrived, Maria had called the office and Horace told me. I got here about an hour ago."

"Maria, thank you!" Graciella said. "But how. . .why. . .?"

"We let you sleep," Maria interrupted, "because you needed it. The doctor is making rounds now. He should be in any minute."

As if on cue, the door opened and a heavy-set Hispanic man with graying hair and moustache entered. He wore slacks, a Western short-sleeved shirt, and bola tie with a turquoise and silver slide. A stethoscope was hooked around his neck. "Good afternoon," he smiled at all present. "Hello, Maria," he said, recognizing her.

"Hello, Doctor," she said. "Your patient is anxious," she gestured towards Graciella, "so we'll wait outside." Maria and Greg left the room.

"I'm Doctor Trujillo," he smiled perfunctorily, reaching for her chart at the foot of the bed. He pulled up a chair and sat beside her. "I guess you have quite a headache."

She nodded, "A big one! Am I all right?"

"Oh, I think so," he said, "but let me just make sure." He said nothing more, nor did she, for the next several minutes while he took pulse and blood pressure, listened to her heart, and inspected each of her bandages. It turned out that she also had a bandage on her right shin, an injury she had not noticed. He finally examined her eyes, testing convergence and dilation.

"Well," he sat back, looking at her. "You will be sore for awhile, but you are very lucky." He scribbled on her chart. "Very lucky, yes sir." He looked up. "No serious or permanent damage."

"When can I leave?" asked Graciella.

"Well. . . ," he paused, "it would be wise for us to observe you overnight, but," his eyes sparkled, "you probably would not like our food. If you promise to rest in bed until tomorrow and take no alcohol or drugs, I'll let you go." He rose. "But you must call if you feel any worse."

"Oh, I promise," Graciella tried to laugh. She started to sit up.

"No, not yet," Dr. Trujillo restrained her. "The nurse will come in to help while your friends sign you out." He patted her arm. "You be careful, now," he said, and left with her chart.

After a few minutes, another nurse, a heavyset Anglo, came in to help her, bringing a wheelchair. When she had dressed, Graciella sat in the wheelchair. "I'd like to say goodbye to nurse Lujan," she said. "Is she around?"

"Who?" asked the nurse.

"Lujan," Graciella looked at her. "Her name tag read 'A. Lujan'. She was short, Indian, long black hair."

The nurse looked back at her quizzically. "Ma'am, we have no Lujan on our staff," she said. "Only six of us here right now, and no-one fits that description."

How strange, thought Graciella. But I was just waking, and with this knockout headache. Could I have hallucinated?

Greg and Maria checked her out, and she and Maria had driven back to the Fort with Greg following in his rental car. Maria had urged Graciella to spend the night in the spare bedroom of the Commander's Quarters, and Greg had offered the spare bedroom in his apartment. She had insisted, however, on staying in her own apartment. They had agreed, with the proviso that Maria would bring her dinner and Greg would check in from time to time before going to bed.

When they returned they found that Ned had retrieved her Explorer and all of her gear. She thanked Ned and he asked about her condition, which she assured him was okay. "Really, I look worse than I am." Felix stood to one side as Maria and Greg helped Graciella through the door, a worried—almost angry—frown on his brow. She smiled at him, "I'll be fine, Felix."

Horace was in her apartment turning down the bed. "Now, Grace," he said in his typical gruff voice, "you tell us what you need. We'll make sure you're comfortable."

"Thank you, Dr. Stern," she said. "I'm just happy to be back here in one piece." Maria helped her to the bed, then shooed everyone out. "Leave us," she said. "I can help her from here on. Horace, go to the Dining Hall. Get them to fix some hot soup. Bring it in a covered pan with tortillas."

When they were alone, Maria helped Graciella get into a long gown and bathrobe and fixed a pillow bolster so she could sit up comfortably in bed. Maria pulled up a chair. "We will wait for Horace and the soup. How is your headache?"

"It hurts," said Graciella. She fixed Maria with a stare. "Maria, you took me to the hospital. You must have found me. Tell me how you knew."

Maria looked at her solemnly for a moment. "I heard your scream, Graciella. It was most terrifying. I was across the road, where the art students were packing their canvases. I drove immediately to the site. You were wedged in the debris, between a wall and the floor."

Graciella continued looking at her. "I guess it is fortunate that I screamed so loud," she said.

Maria smiled slightly. "You are fortunate in many ways, Graciella, but also sometimes foolhardy." She leaned forward. "You are a driven soul these past months. I think it is dangerous."

"Let's not speak in riddles, Maria," Graciella said. "Tell me what you mean."

"You are headstrong, Graciella," Maria said softly. "If this excavation had proceeded normally, during next field season, these mishaps would have been avoided."

Graciella frowned. "Are you suggesting that whoever filled in my excavation would have been less intent to stop me next season?"

"I think next season you would have not been digging here," Maria said. "You would be finishing your field research elsewhere. Remember? You said this was your last chance."

Yes, Graciella remembered. Greg had told her that next season she should plan on travelling around the region, visiting other sites and contemporary pueblos to make final comparisons before analysis and writing. "So," Graciella said cautiously, "you think that the person responsible was specifically against _me_ doing the excavation." She shook her head. "I've gone over all of the potential suspects many times, Maria, and there is simply no one who would stand to gain by preventing me from excavating."

Maria sat for a moment, thinking. Then, apparently having concluded a debate with herself, said softly, "Graciella, let me tell you a story; a true story." She sat straight in the chair, hands on her knees. "Several years ago, in our field biology course, the professor had the students set out live traps, overnight, for rodents. These are small aluminum boxes, called Sherman traps. The next morning the traps were collected and each rodent—deer mouse, field mouse, kangaroo rat—was tagged and let loose. This was near the beginning of the term. At the end of the term traps were set out again, and they counted the next morning to see how many tagged animals were caught a second time."

Graciella said, "I know, Maria; this is routine censusing. They do it every year."

"Yes," said Maria, "but not the same way any more. Back then, while students were told to collect their traps early, some didn't get to them before the sun was up. Many animals were dead from the heat, or from the ants which become active hunters at dawn." Graciella shifted uncomfortably at the thought.

"There was one student who could not abide this," Maria continued. "The thought of the tiny mice being eaten while they were alive, or baking in their little aluminum ovens, was too much. She fretted about it all term. Then, at the end of the term, the traps were once again set out at night."

Maria paused for effect. "At dawn the next morning, the traps were collected. All were empty. Every one." Maria leaned forward slightly and looked at Graciella directly. "Listen to what I'm saying, Graciella," she almost whispered. "The student did not do this out of rancor, nor from jealousy, nor out of any ill feelings toward the professor or the students. It was no practical joke. It was done to protect the animals."

The two women sat silently for awhile, looking at each other. Finally, Graciella closed her eyes and turned her head. "You believe that someone is trying to protect the site? From me?"

Suddenly, the visions she had been having, the dream the other night, the strange and sometimes very uncomfortable feelings she experienced, all came back to her in this one and singular idea. At one level she had been resisting such a conclusion. At another level, she had wanted desperately to share it, have it independently confirmed or dismissed.

Graciella had long been ambiguous on this issue. To open it up for inspection would lift a source of some mental torment, but at the risk of exposing her fragile sanity. To safeguard it for introspection would allow her to retain the possibility that its reality was fragmentary at worst and fabricated entirely at best, but keeping it within her reinforced the uncertainty.

Her eyes were moist as she opened them on Maria. ". . .To protect the site from me alone, but not from others?" Both Nurse Lujan and Felix had warned her about working alone.

Maria placed her hand on Graciella's. "Think of what has happened in the past year. Your first experience at the site; your new name; your uncharacteristic melancholy; your obvious obsession with that room and what lies beneath it. It would not be farfetched for someone to see a special link between you and that site; to want to break that link."

"What do you believe, Maria?" Graciella placed her other hand on Maria's and squeezed it. "Am I becoming mad? What is happening?"

The creaking of boards underfoot in the hallway outside announced, for Graciella, an unwelcome intrusion. A light knock on the door. "We'll talk later," whispered Maria. She arose and opened the door. Horace entered with a small cast-iron camp kettle, and a large folded cloth.

"Ladies," he announced, "I bear the native cure of all ills—grippe, diarrhea, the black bile, and headaches from adobe walls. Arguella's infamous and inflammable green chili stew!" He placed the kettle on the stovetop.

"Colorfully misinterpreted, Husband," said Maria, rising to get bowl and spoon. "Chili is a hot food, to balance the cooler humours. Nevertheless, it should serve its purpose for Graciella." She set the table, poured some milk from the refrigerator, ladled some soup into the bowl, and set the folded cloth containing warm tortillas beside the plate. "Now," she said, moving to help Graciella up, "some food in your stomach should help dispel your headache."

Graciella sat at the table. "Thank you both," she said. "I am feeling better despite the headache. Hungry, too. Dr. Stern," she turned to him, "what about the site. What will happen there?"

"Tomorrow, my dear," he patted her on the shoulder. "As Ms. Mitchell wrote, we'll worry about that tomorrow. Greg and I—and you, if you're feeling better—shall inspect the damage and together reach a decision."

"Come, Horace," Maria took his arm. "We'll let Graciella dine and slumber." She turned to Graciella. "Greg will look in on you later."

"Maria," said Graciella, "what happened to the student?"

Maria paused in the doorway. "The one who released the traps? They never found out who she was."

"Really?" asked Graciella. "How do they know it was a 'she'?"

Maria gave her a wry look. "They don't know," she said. "I know." She paused with her hand on the doorknob. "Let's keep it as our little secret: I was that student. Goodnight." She closed the door.

Graciella was able to think more clearly as she ate. The chili soup—actually it was more like a stew, with its boiled potatoes and onions and chunks of chili meat—was indeed diminishing her headache. She realized she had not eaten since seven that morning, and had a second bowl and three glasses of milk plus an additional tortilla before climbing back into bed.

There was so much yet to understand, she thought. Now, at least, perhaps she could share some things with Maria. That would be safe. Maria had not told her what <u>she</u> believed about the site. She remembered now the conversation with Nurse Lujan, whoever she was, at Holy Cross. She had said the same thing: she was in the wrong place. <u>She</u>, Graciella. . .not just anyone. Is that what she meant? Is that what Maria meant?

From the beginning, Graciella had felt something personal between her and Room 703. For over a year the feeling had grown, building with each of the several events. She had confided in no one. Now, it appears, Maria somehow had known. And A. Lujan.

And, Graciella reflected as she began to doze off, the person intent on stopping her had known. In her compromised state, she wondered whether the collapse and her fall were due to gravity acting above or a vacuum acting below. Some spirit pushing her down, or some other pulling her in? What a strange concept, she thought. Almost humorous. A Dr. Seuss story.

When Greg knocked lightly on her door and looked in quietly, Graciella was asleep, breathing deeply. It was only eight-thirty.

7

Graciella awakened at six. It had been, apparently, a quiet, restful night. The long hours of sleep had restored the flagging spirit that had been deprived of energy these past few days by tension and apprehension. Her headache was gone, she realized as she lay awake in bed. She felt completely rested and recharged. She inhaled deeply.

Juniper berries. The scent filled the room. She knew instantly that it was going to happen again, and for the third time. A peaceful, floating sensation and a slow transition of awareness from her immediate surroundings to those of some earlier time. Then pungent sage and an awareness, that was both visual and non-sensory, of details normally hidden. As before, there was no feeling of anxiety, no hesitation in the transition. Neither was there the sense of motion or shift of consciousness which occurs when entering a trance.

As before, there was recognition of the familiar in the remote. What had been impersonal and distant became personal and present, and Graciella silently acknowledged the roles of juniper and sage—the former as vehicle for the transition, the latter as vehicle for awareness. She understood it, welcomed it, and awaited the completion of the transition to a flowing, almost poetic reality for which there was no map, nor any guide.

◇◇◇

Gather, kin of Clan Ayutl, turtle kinsmen, circle here.
Here our daughter, Graciella, of our winter people's kin—
of the Eagle Clan—is injured. Sing, 'Atoya, bring her close.
Quickly, she is with us only shortly, now is strengthened
by her rest and by the food she took at sundown. Seek protection while we work;
seek defense behind the hillside.
Toc-a-pilli, bring the cure. See, her blood is all but drying,
all congealing, disappearing—Patecatl, god of curing,
needs fresh blood to mix the poultice. Hurry! Blend the best ezpatli.

Calmly, now, I watch their movements as they bathe the wounds and fan them,
cooling with a breath of winter in this summer's burning heat.
Am I thinking of the danger from the A-ten-calli people?
They are us, and with our history they have shared the sacred path,
yet still they create ill among us. There's some truth I cannot see.
Toc-a-pilli has the essence, now applies it with each chant
as young Tlatoya sings the sequence. First, a brush of flower pollen —
"Xochinochtli" is the chant—and a paste of maize and water,
and another application I cannot identify.
At last a covering of resin, "ocotzotl" in the song,
that smells of pine, a hint of pinyon, and a leaf tied 'round to hold it.
This for each of four abrasions, each with chant and whispered words,
and now it's over. I lie hidden, on petlatl by a stream, looking out beyond the forest.
Three protectors, not too far,
but glancing back each twenty heartbeats. Out beyond, I see the houses,
stacked like clouds above the terrace, bright as corn beneath the sunlight. . .
peace and beauty fill my spirit. . .eagle circles far above,
in a sleepy spiral downward. . .heavy eyelids close my vision. . .close. . . .
Sleep, my daughter, Huetxochitl, safe until our next encounter. . .
faintly, voices closed to hearing. . . . Finally, not a sound remaining.
Scent of sage begins to fade, now. Juniper and sage together. . .
all but gone. Now closed to fragrance. . .
gone. . . .
Only darkness to my vision, only silence to my hearing,
not a fragrance, nothing tactile. Only thoughts, like colors, streaming
and cascading and informing.

◇◇◇

". . .and I haven't been able to awaken her. She breathes steadily; the pulse seems strong. Is she in a coma?" Graciella heard, faintly at first and then more loudly the agitated voice of Greg Parson. He was breathing heavily, as if he had been running.

She opened her eyes. Maria was bending over her, in the process of taking her pulse. Behind her stood Greg, a frantic look on his face, and next to him was Horace.

"What's the matter?" asked Graciella, sleepily.

Greg expelled his breath in a loud sigh. "My God, Grace, I thought you were gone! I came in, tried to wake you up, and got no response." He smiled in relief. "I mean, lady, I <u>shook</u> you enough to wake the dead."

"He came running to us, white as a sheet," said Maria. She dropped Graciella's wrist. "Pulse is 92," she said. "Strong." She stood and turned to the men. "She's perfectly fine."

"What time is it?" asked Graciella.

"Eight-ten," said Horace. "Morning. Grace, how do you feel? How is your head?"

"I feel totally rested," said Grace, smiling. "Headache is gone. Even my scrapes don't hurt," she reached up, touching the bandage on her temple.

Greg shook his head. "I just don't see <u>how</u> you could have been sleeping so soundly!" He smiled at her, "But I'm sure glad you're okay."

"Let's leave this young lady to get dressed," said Horace. He turned to her. "When you're up to it, come to our place for coffee. You and Greg and I will visit, then we'll drive over to the site and inspect everything."

"Okay," said Graciella. "I'll take a quick shower and join you." She looked at Greg, smiling. "Sorry I worried you, but I'm fine."

The three of them left. Graciella sat on the edge of the bed for a moment. "Good lord!" she thought. She remembered, as she always did, every detail of her—dream? Vision? Journey? Which was it?—and, as before, there was left within her a residue of soft, mellow feelings. What convinced her that this, and the two others, were more than mere dreams was the fact that she not only remembered them well, but trivial details, including sounds, smells, sights, were in sharp focus. "Good lord!" she said aloud. She would spend some time recording this on tape. She had done the same with the other two such incidents.

She undressed and turned on the shower. I guess I'd better check these bandages, she thought. I can avoid getting the head dressing wet, but certainly not the other three. Perhaps, she thought, she should just take a sponge bath.

She carefully pulled the tape off one end of the gauze dressing on her wrist and folded it back. She stared at it as her heart raced momentarily. Where was the wound? She pulled off the gauze. There was no scrape, no abrasion, not a single scratch! She looked in the mirror and did the same with the dressing on her temple. Not a sign of any damage there, either!

"Oh, my God," she said softly. She did not have to remove the other two bandages to know that the same results would be seen there. She put her elbows on her knees, resting her head in her hands.

As she did so, she detected, from her right wrist, the slightest aroma of turpentine. Resin. Pine resin. . .*ocotzotl*!

"Oh, my God," she said again. She wept silently as complex emotions sent signals through her stomach and into her throat. Her tears were neither of sadness, nor of fear, nor even of happiness. She had never before been so confused, and yet so strangely peaceful.

8

"More coffee?" Maria gestured to Greg, seated across from Horace at the breakfast table in their quarters. The morning sun stroked harshly through the kitchen window and diffused into the breakfast room.

"Yes, please," Greg replied, absently. He glanced at his watch—eight forty—and folded his arms on the table. He and Horace had been discussing the latest distressing turn of events. "Horace, I have no problem with your authorization for the backhoe. Grace is perfectly competent." He looked up at Horace. "Particularly," he said, "since you insisted that Felix be there with her."

Horace smiled. "I checked with Felix afterwards," he said. "He said she handled it like a surgeon wields a scalpel." He paused. "Well, those were not his exact words, of course, but he was quite impressed." He stroked his goatee and leaned back as Maria poured his coffee. "Thanks, Love," he glanced at her.

"How long did Felix stay with her?" Maria asked Horace. She had put the carafe down and returned to the kitchen for hot tea, which she preferred.

"I believe he left with the backhoe as soon as she finished," Horace said. "By the way, Greg," he said, "Felix said she was finished inside of fifteen minutes of putting that machine in position."

"She's very good with it," Greg said. "Lots of experience. Have you been over there since it happened?"

"No," said Horace. "When Maria called from the hospital, I was down at the geology lab with Ned. Karen put the call through. Ned volunteered to go get Grace's Explorer. I don't know whether he actually climbed the mound or not." He looked at Greg. "Have you been to the site?"

"No," Greg shook his head. "After we brought Grace back from the hospital, I unpacked and went to the Dining Hall. Danny and Andy were there, and we talked until almost seven. Then I came back to check on Grace."

"Well, I didn't hear you," Graciella said, entering from the kitchen door. "And I obviously didn't hear you this morning when you tried to wake me up." She sat in the fourth place, between the two men at opposite ends of the rectangular table. She smiled up at Maria as she accepted a cup of hot coffee. "I'm really sorry if my deep sleep frightened you." A sidelong glance at Maria revealed no change of expression. Did she know?

"'Deep sleep' is not the word for it, friend," Greg chuckled. "I still can't believe you were so far under!"

"Has anyone been to the site?" Graciella asked. "I wonder how much damage was done."

"We were just discussing that," said Greg. "But a fallen wall can't be too serious. We'll just remove it and go on," he smiled at her.

She frowned, looking at Greg, then Horace. Perplexed, she turned to Maria, who was sipping her tea. "A fallen wall? Maria, didn't you tell them about the damage?"

"I'm sorry, Graciella," she looked up. "I told Horace, but I haven't seen Greg long enough to explain."

"Explain what?" Greg looked up quizzically. "Didn't a wall fall in?"

"Yes," said Graciella, "it did. It fell because the floor collapsed under me and pulled the wall with it!"

"Floor collapsed?" Greg looked confused. "How could a floor collapse?"

"It collapsed into the underlying kiva," said Graciella.

"Impossible!" Greg said. "The debris of that mound has been untouched for over six hundred years! How could it suddenly collapse?"

"Exactly," Graciella said. "I think you are about to be very surprised, Greg." She grasped her cup, feeling its warmth conveyed into both of her hands. "I most sincerely hope you can find a rational explanation."

Greg was now very interested. He put both palms on the table as he stood. "Well," he said. "Let's just see this impossibility!"

◇◇◇

The four of them drove over to Pot Creek in Graciella's vehicle, as Ned had taken the Center's Bronco that morning. They left a trail of dust despite the light rain the previous night. As they parked, Graciella again saw the circling scavengers above. Did they never leave, she wondered?

At the top of Unit VII they slowly spread out along the periphery of what yesterday morning had been a clean excavation of Room 703. The floor, what could be seen of it, tilted down at a forty-degree angle and was cracked apart across this incline. The basin had broken apart and its circular adobe curb tilted up where fragments still clung to the floor. The south end of the floor, its highest part, had sunken about six inches to a depth of four feet from the mound surface. It also tilted downward slightly toward the east, but the south wall was still intact. Its nine-foot length was canted a few degrees to the north, but the unexcavated fill from its top surface southward had not pushed it over.

The east and west walls—defining the narrow dimension of the rectangular room—were tilted down following the floor, although their slant did not quite equal that of the floor from which these walls had become detached. Parts of the east wall, the most sharply angled, had broken away from the back-fill that still protected Room 704, and fragments of adobe had fallen into the room.

The north wall, however, had been subject to the most severe stress. Adobe wall construction in this 14th Century pueblo had been laid in horizontal layers, or courses. Each course, nearly a foot thick and varying from 16 to 20 inches in height, had been laid down as a continuous structure, rounded on top. When dried, the next course was laid. Most rooms originally had four such courses, with the roof/floor timbers inserted in the fourth course. The center post had supported a single viga, running the length of the room. Across this viga had been laid smaller *latillas*. The single viga spanning a 5 ft by 9 ft room lengthwise therefore reduced the unsupported width from 5 to 2-1/2 feet. This span required only small latillas—covered by straw and brush, then adobe—to support human weight on the surface above. Centerposts for upper floor rooms could be shaped to fit over the viga below and to support the viga above; hence each center post above the lowest one—that was often placed two feet into the ground—was the exact height of the room. With such construction, contiguous rooms sharing common walls could be stacked vertically to four stories with little danger of collapse. This construction style was unique to the prehistoric Taos region: standing ruins at Picuris and Taos Pueblos displayed the same feature, but nowhere else was it found.

The flaw in such structural design, however, lay in the critical importance of the center post. These had to be absolutely vertical to support the stress of the viga, acting as it were like a middle wall in a 9-foot room span. A slight movement off-vertical, as when a previously abandoned room began to settle, could spell disaster for all rooms above. It was hypothesized that this danger led to the change in construction following Spanish influence after 1640.

At Pot Creek, only ground-floor rooms had been preserved, and upper floor rooms, where originally present, had simply crumbled and collapsed like a house of cards into the lower rooms. The best preserved rooms, ironically, were those originally supporting three and four stories. Because these were commonly in the center of room blocks, collapse onto and into these central rooms had been partially protected by the strength of surrounding structures.

Room 703 had been such a room. The standing north wall, when excavated, had stood just under 5 feet. Its coursed adobe construction, with adobe plaster coating intact on much of its surface, had all four courses preserved.

Excavation originally had revealed an eight degree dip in the floor toward north, and a similar tilt of the north wall away from vertical. Since the room abutting 703 and sharing this north wall had not been excavated, the wall could not move further off-vertical.

Now, however, the floor, broken as it was and canting forty degrees downward, had pulled the lower two adobe wall courses with it, but had forced the upper two courses to straighten as it sank and finally to topple into the room in large fragments. It had been this that collapsed onto Graciella, and a broken fragment had knocked her unconscious.

The bottom-most third of this fall—where the north wall had collapsed—was now obscured by numerous dried rabbit-brush plants which, as tumbleweeds, had been blown into the cavity. What could be seen, however, was more than enough to draw whistles of disbelief from Greg and Horace.

"Good Lord," said Horace, walking back and forth and peering downward, "I never imagined this kind of damage when Maria described it." He shook his head. "Good Lord!"

Greg was hunkered down, elbows on his knees, peering into the pit. "Maria, I don't know how you got Grace out of here by yourself! This is one deep sink."

"It wasn't this deep!" exclaimed Maria. "It must have settled at least another foot or more since I got her out." Maria walked around toward the east side. "Yes," she said, "I stepped down here easily, then moved a fragment of fallen wall to reach Graciella."

Graciella stared at the pit, transfixed by the evidence of such great destruction, trying to remember the collapse. "Maria's right," said Grace. "I'm positive the depth was not nearly as much as this when it happened." Although the chamisa blocked the view, the depth that was visible extended six feet from the surface. Add another three feet, thought Graciella, if you remove the brush.

Greg walked around to join Maria on the east side. "I can't believe it's this deep simply from collapsing into an unexcavated kiva!" he exclaimed. "This is absolutely inexplicable!"

"Greg," said Graciella, "I took a profile of the east wall the night before last and again the next morning. It had moved half a degree in a few short hours! Believe me," she shook her head, "this was dynamic from the beginning!"

"And maybe still is," he said, leaning down, on hands and knees, peering into the brush. "Grace, you leave something down there?"

"Probably my trowel and hand mattock," she said. "My trowel was on the floor, and my strike with the pick caused all of this."

"Well, there's something white down under the brush," he said. He got up, searched around the mound, and went down the far side into a depression where a juniper was growing. He returned with a short length of dead juniper limb. Lying on his stomach and reaching down with the stick, he could easily reach the chamisa. He began fishing the top bush out of the way, finally flicking it up over the west end of the collapse. "Hey. . .what. . . ," Greg stammered. He hastily reached down again, probing for another bush, finally caught it and moved it aside. "Jesus!" he cried, pulling the limb back.

Barely revealed in the shadows of the deepest part, and still mostly covered by rabbit-brush, was a body, very still. Wearing something white.

"Oh, Lord," said Horace. "Who is it? Can we get down there?"

"I'm light," said Maria. "Horace, hold onto my arm. Maybe I can get down far enough to at least take a pulse! Hurry!" Horace and Greg together held onto Maria while she gingerly stepped into the collapsed area and tested the broken floor for support. It held with no sign of movement. "Lower me a bit more," Maria said.

"Be careful, Love," said Horace. "Don't go any deeper; we can't hold you."

"Just a fraction more," she said. With her free hand she pulled out much of the rest of the brush. The body—a woman—was lying face down, lengthwise along the axis of the lower course of the north wall. Portions of the upper, fallen courses of the north wall covered her lower torso. One arm was up next to her head, the other was hidden beneath her.

Maria reached out and was able to grasp the wrist of the exposed arm. "Okay," she said. "Just hold me still a moment." The moment became an eternity, and Graciella, standing mute the entire time, felt as if she must pass out. She went to her knees, put her head down onto the ground, and breathed deeply.

"Help me out," said Maria. The men had her up and out immediately. "Dead," she said. "Cold. Rigor mortis."

Horace reached out and encircled her with his arms. "Could you see the face, Love? Could you identify her?"

"No," Maria shuddered. "Hispanic, I believe. Young. Not one of our students. I don't believe she is one of our staff." She buried her face in his shoulder.

"I'll drive to the office and call the sheriff and ambulance," Greg said. "Grace, are you all right? You'd better come with me."

"No, go," Graciella replied, her head still low and not looking at him. "I must stay here! We all must! Go quickly!"

"Yes," said Horace. "We'll wait down by the trees."

Greg ran to the Explorer, in a minute was spinning wheels down the rutted dirt road, leaving clouds of dust. The other three walked down to the junipers and pinyon encircling Pot Creek Pueblo, sat in the shade on soft needles, and waited. They spoke little.

◇◇◇

It seemed forever, but actually took less than twenty minutes. The sirens in the distance grew closer and louder. The deputy sheriff's car followed Greg, who had waited at the highway, and the ambulance followed last.

The deputy sheriff, a burly Hispanic with black moustache on a young, slightly pock-marked face, climbed the mound behind Greg. Graciella, Horace and Maria followed. Behind them came two white-clad paramedics. All circled around the scene at Room 703. "Do you know who she is?" asked the deputy. His name tag, above his badge, read *Pete Montoya*.

"No," said Horace, "but we can't see her face. We're reasonably sure she's a stranger."

"I checked for a pulse," said Maria. "I'm a nurse at the Pueblo. She's cold; probably been dead some time."

"Boys," Pete Montoya gestured to the paramedics, "we gotta get her out of there."

"Careful," said Greg. "The site is very unstable. There's loose soil below her and the whole surface has been slowly sinking."

"We've got a harness," one of them said. The other returned to the ambulance for equipment. "Officer Montoya," he asked, "do you want to move it before detectives see it?"

Montoya looked at him. "Well, Chuck," he said slowly, "we need detectives if we got a crime scene here. We don't know if we have or not. Got to move her to determine that." He looked at Greg. "Man here says be careful. Get her out."

He turned to the others. "Soon's they have her up here, we'll see if she's familiar to any of you, or if there's a purse down there with I.D.," he said. "Then I'll be wanting to get all your names and details about this place."

They all stood together, except officer Montoya, as the men worked gingerly with the ropes, harness, and a gurney they had brought to the edge. No one said anything. All were transfixed by the scene below, waiting expectantly. Even Pete Montoya watched with intense curiosity as, ever so carefully, the body was placed in the harness and ropes were attached. The men below worked methodically, needing only occasional communication. The rubble moved little and the surface below appeared solid, for the moment, as they worked. A heavy rubber sheet was wrapped around the body to protect it from any postmortem abrasions. Finally, with one pulling from above and the other lifting from below, the two men raised the woman to the surface.

Graciella shuddered, hugging herself with her arms. "I can't believe this, she's exactly where I was lying yesterday," she whispered.

"You?" said Pete Montoya. "You were in this pit?"

"She caused it to collapse," Horace said. "On top of her."

"On top. . . ." Montoya began.

"Which is why she was in Holy Cross," said Maria. Graciella looked very pale to her. "Excuse me, I must get her some water." Maria walked down towards the Explorer to fetch Graciella's canteen, which she had noticed on the ride over.

"Yesterday, you said?" Montoya removed his hat and wiped his brow. The two paramedics had now cleared the wall with the wrapped body and put it on the gurney. They carefully unwrapped the rubber sheet and lifted away the portion covering the face.

All of them looked down at the face. An attractive Indian girl, probably around twenty, oval but not plump face, high cheekbones. Long, black hair.

"Not a staff worker," said Horace, as Maria grabbed his shoulder and thrust her right hand to her mouth in shock.

"Never saw her," said Greg, "as far as I know. Grace?" he turned to her.

Graciella moved closer. "My God! Nurse Lujan!" she said, grasping Greg's arm.

All turned to look at Graciella, who had turned pale. "Lujan," said Montoya. "A nurse. You know her."

"In the hospital," said Graciella, weakly. "In a uniform, but not a nurse."

"Not a nurse?"

"Not a nurse. But with a name tag: *A. Lujan*. Yesterday."

A small crowd had now gathered nearby: Ned, two of the students, Karen Brown, two of the workers. All had followed the sound of the sirens, and were now in a small group, speaking in hushed voices.

The paramedics had unfolded the remainder of the sheet. On the white uniform, left side, was a blue plastic name tag: 'A. Lujan' was incised on it, in white letters. Officer Montoya knelt down and looked at it.

Just about three inches below this badge was a dark stain. It surrounded and had spread laterally from a diagonal tear in the fabric, about 2-1/2 inches long. Just about the position of the fifth intercostal—between the fifth and sixth ribs.

Officer Montoya looked at this, too, and then at Graciella. And then at the others. He rose with a deliberate slowness. He put his thumbs in his belt, just below a slightly enlarged belly. As Maria approached with the canteen, he carefully looked at each of the three people standing and facing him.

"Okay, folks," he said in a rising voice. "Now we got ourselves a crime scene. Here's the way we're going to play this." He deliberately looked again at each. "I'm gonna walk down there to that patrol car," he pointed toward it. "I'm gonna call one of our homicide detectives, and he's gonna call the medical examiner."

Officer Montoya took a deep breath, then let it out slowly. "Then," he said, "I'm gonna come back up here, and each of you, you and me's gonna have a little talk. We're gonna talk about holes that put people in hospitals one day and hide murder victims the next. We're gonna talk about nurses in hospitals that ain't nurses and that don't work in hospitals."

Officer Montoya looked at the crowd. "Alright, people," he announced loudly, "now you folks just be sure and stay back from this hilltop here. We got more officers coming." He turned to the paramedics. "Boys, cover her back up and stay put. We got physical evidence all around us here. Nobody move."

He gave Graciella, Greg, Horace and Maria his most serious and sternest look. "Nobody move," he repeated.

Then Pete Montoya walked down the mound towards the still rotating lights of his patrol car. This was going to be a very long day for paperwork, he thought. Probably make less sense with each statement, he thought. What's worse, he said to himself, these people are probably from Goddamn Texas.

9

Detective Ben Sandoval had finished his preliminary interviews with each of the four, taking notes on a small pad. Pete Montoya, meanwhile, had taken names and statements from the small group of onlookers. Sandoval and Montoya were now conferring next to the body. The medical examiner, kneeling, was completing his own examination.

"All these people here are with the research center," Montoya was saying. "They say they didn't know nothing about this until they heard my siren, Lieutenant." He looked at his notes. "I got all their names. Some live here—in Talpa and Ranchos—and work at the center. Most are just here for the summer." He looked over the small group. "From Texas," he said.

"Okay, Pete," Detective Sandoval said. "I'll need to compare your notes with mine on these four. You follow the body back and get your report done." He looked down at the body. "What about it, Doc?" he asked. "You got time and cause of death, yet?"

"Only preliminary," the Medical Examiner looked up. To the two para-medics he said, "Okay, boys. Take it back with you and tell them to prepare for autopsy." He closed his bag and stood. "The victim died most likely from a puncture wound—you saw it," he said to Sandoval. "Manner is likely homicide. Probably a knife. She's probably been dead between sixteen and eighteen hours. There's still some rigor."

Sandoval did some mental calculations. "Around mid-afternoon yester-day," he said. "She was seen at the hospital around two, two-thirty. You think she was killed here or somewhere else?"

"Probably here," the examiner nodded towards the collapsed room, where an officer was gingerly checking the debris. "There's no lividity in the gluteal area and back of the legs; more on the left front side than right. Fits with the position you say she was in. You found her face down, right?"

"That's right, Doc, but more on her left side," Pete Montoya said.

"I'll know more after the autopsy," the Medical Examiner said, as the three began moving toward the vehicles. "You be sure to notify next of kin right away," he said. "I want to start this after lunch." Autopsy on a homicide victim required no permission from kin, but notification was important—especially in a small community like this, where word would spread out of Holy Cross rapidly. And especially for an Indian girl.

"I'll take care of that," Sandoval said. "Pete, I'll check with you later." Sandoval watched the examiner and Montoya leave, then dismissed all the onlookers with the understanding that they would not leave the region without notifying him. He walked back up the mound and stood staring at the depression, which had already settled even deeper. This was going to be a very curious case, he thought.

Ben Sandoval was Apache. He had grown up on the Jicarilla Reservation west of the San Juan range, across the Taos Plateau. His father had been a horse breeder and trader, and Ben had grown up with a love of the outdoors and an abiding interest in people. The variety who had come to do business with his father—Indian, Hispanic, Anglo—had an equal variety of techniques for negotiating and skills in making trades. His father, an astute and intelligent man whose uniform approach was as a stoic listener—you can learn more from listening than from talking, he used to say—had taught him the art of reading people and their motives.

Ben had attended the University of Colorado on scholarship and graduated with a criminal justice major. Four years on the Albuquerque police force had taught him two things: the U.S. criminal justice system is less effective than the Apache way, and a high plateau Indian could not easily adapt to the desert heat of the southern Rio Grande.

He had consequently spent two years back on the reservation as a Tribal Policeman, a job as comforting in its security as it was unchallenging in its predictability. He had taken the Taos job two years ago, just recently passed the detective exams and now, at 36, was genuinely enjoying the work and its variety.

He wore his black hair parted in the middle, the shoulder-length braids framing a narrow, rather craggy face with projecting cheekbones. Many women found him ruggedly handsome, the more so because of his inherited quiet, impassive demeanor. Ben Sandoval was unmarried, however, and not seeking any romantic involvement. Much like Greg Parson, from whom he was otherwise profoundly different, his work was all-consuming.

Now, he stood atop Unit VII deep in thought. The man below was carefully inspecting the surface where the body had been found. Ben wished Pete had not had the body moved. Too many details forensics can lose when the context is changed. Even so, blood at the scene agreed with the M.E.'s opinion. Why had the victim been here? Why had she been at Holy Cross? What was the connection? Ben remembered a cardinal rule of criminal investigation: there are no coincidences.

Maria Stern had recognized the victim as a volunteer at the Pueblo Clinic—Anita Lujan. She was a member of the pueblo. Too many threads of circumstance were connected to this location: the student, Grace, had been injured here, taken to the hospital by Maria, who worked with the victim at the pueblo. The victim appears in the hospital room as a nurse, but turns up here, at the site of the student's accident, dead. At the center where Maria's husband is director. He shook his head. There are no coincidences.

◇◇◇

Taos Pueblo is a monument to austerity. Its small adobe rooms sit atop one another in upwardly decreasing tiers. The somewhat imprecise arrangement reminds one of casually stacked children's blocks. The walls are stark and simple in their rectilinear surfaces and softly contoured edges. Their earth-colored hues mirror those of the vast plaza below, while the blue-framed windows and doors offer counterpoint to the vast sky above. If a place could be both humble and commanding at the same time, Taos Pueblo would define it.

Ben Sandoval approached it from its public road on the south. While only two miles north of town, it's distance in cultural tradition was immeasurable. Ben had called ahead, without relating the nature of the matter, and had been reminded that most of the members were gone. The annual pilgrimage to the sacred Blue Lake is held each August, where for three days in ceremony adolescent boys are initiated into their kiva societies and the pueblo celebrates a renewal of life.

The Lieutenant Governor, or pueblo "sheriff", had not yet left, fortunately, and would see Sandoval before taking the trek. Sandoval knew the Lieutenant Governor, Antonio Romero, although only casually. He tried to predict his—and the pueblo's—reaction to this, particularly during the August ceremonies.

Ben parked his Toyota pickup next to the church at the pueblo entrance. Romero approached from across the plaza as Ben got out. He was a short, rotund man in his late-fifties, Ben guessed, hair in braids and wearing the traditional denim jeans, with a blanket wrapped around his middle and gathered up to cover his head.

They shook hands. "Haven't seen you in awhile, Ben," Romero said. "I guess this is official business. August 24th is not a normal time for visiting."

Ben gave him a guilty look. "Actually, Tony, I forgot the date," he said, "but it is official." He looked around. "Where can we talk?"

Romero gestured towards the plaza. "Let's walk," he said.

They began walking towards the Rio Pueblo. The river—a large stream at this point—was fed by Blue Lake, miles away, and split the pueblo community into two architectural clusters. The north pueblo, to their left, had the large contiguous room blocks which gave rise to four stories—five in one case. The south pueblo was essentially the same size, but with rooms in more linear arrangements, and with fewer stories.

Tony Romero looked up to the distant mountains which rose out of the sagebrush flats rather precipitously about ten miles north, and which framed almost the entire northern horizon. "They are there, by now," he indicated with a nod towards Taos Mountain. It shimmered in the heat rising off the distant plain, coated in the green of conifers for most of its height. Its peak, like a mythical Mt. Olympus, lay bared and barren in the distance, above the timber line, and no longer wearing the remnant snowy cap which sometimes remains through July. Taos Mountain. *Maw'aluna* in the Tiwa dialect of Taos. Much fought over in contests between the powerful U.S. Congress and the persistent Taos Indians. Much safeguarded now. The sacred mountain. "I will join them this evening," Tony Romero continued, turning towards Ben, "unless you bring reason to stop that trip."

They had passed the first of the three bridges which connected the people of Taos Pueblo across their river—the one known as the American Bridge. They continued in silence for a while, Tony not wishing to know too quickly what brought Ben Sandoval to the pueblo; Ben not wanting to break the quiet of mid-afternoon in the almost empty plaza. As they reached the second bridge, the "earth wood bridge" as the elders knew it, Ben slowed, stopped, and looked at Romero. "Tony," he said, "I bring very sad news, and it may well change your trip to Blue Lake."

As Ben related the details to Tony, as much as he knew them, he watched his face for emotion. It remained somber but unrevealing. When he had finished they both stood in silence: Two Indians, one Apache, still young, born of a nomadic warrior tradition and eager to find and exact retribution; the other, a Taos Indian, no longer in youth, born of a more Apollonian tradition of distrust for outsiders, as anthropologist Ruth Benedict had suggested, but with an uncompromising resolve for self-determination and justice.

"Well," Antonio Romero said, "her mother is here, but her brothers are on the mountain. It will hurt them deeply. Her father, if he were alive, would seek out the witch who killed her." They began walking again, following the river upstream. "Her mother will not take this well," Tony continued. "She's Big Earring People, and I think Anita was, too," he gestured with his chin toward the north pueblo.

They approached the third bridge, now, at the north wall of the village. To their left they could see the projecting ladder posts of the Big Earring Kiva. The two slender aspen timbers shot skyward almost as a taunt to outsiders, who would never know the secrets within but believed them to be grander than they really were. Two women were baking bread in the domed earthen ovens nearby, and three children played next to the pueblo.

Without expression in a face that time and weather had creased, tears welled in Romero's eyes. He coughed back emotion. "Who would have done this, Ben?" he asked. "Who would murder one of our women?"

"I will not rest until we both know, my friend," Ben said softly. "But I need to know everything about Anita: who her friends were, especially boyfriends; where she was yesterday; why she was at Holy Cross; whether she had been troubled or afraid. . . .." He let the words trail off.

"I will have to bring her brothers back down," Tony said, looking at the mountain. Others, too, Ben thought. Burial would have to be soon, traditionally the day after death. And ceremonies, by the Church and by the Pueblo.

Tony turned to Ben. "We will tell her mother when I have brought her sons down. Not alone. I will tell the kiva chiefs, and the War Captain, and the Governor, first." He sighed. "Anita was very important to us," he said, almost as if talking to himself. "She worked at the Clinic, and at the Oo-oona Cultural Arts Center with the children. She was very interested in our heritage, in learning and preserving the old ways."

Tony turned to the low stone and adobe wall that marks the northern boundary of the village. He leaned with his hands on top of it and looked beyond, to the plains and cornfields. "We have a saying about our lives together here, Ben," he said without turning. "'We are in one nest.' Anita appreciated that. As we grow smaller, she wanted to enlarge that nest and keep us together in it."

Ben moved to the wall next to Tony. "Would her interest in your heritage include Pot Creek, Tony?" he asked. "Is there a connection?"

Tony turned to Ben with a frown. "There is," he said. "Legends put our people there, at the two rivers, when the ancient ones emerged from the underworld and became people. But," he waved his hand in dismissal, "there are many legends, and all are different." He raised his hand in caution. "I will tell you this, Ben," he said. "Behind each legend is a seed of truth. Anita was always looking for the truth."

"You think maybe she was close to finding it at Pot Creek, Tony?" asked Ben.

"What I think is not important," Tony said with quiet resolve. "I have a sad journey to make. I will call you when it is done and you can ask questions."

"I'll wait for your call, Tony," Ben said. "I'm very sorry for you and the others." He turned to leave.

"When can we have Anita back?" asked Tony.

"When you are ready for her, we will bring her," Ben answered.

Antonio Romero watched as Ben walked back across the empty plaza. He looked at the tiered adobe rooms and their lengthening afternoon shadows, at the women before their ovens, at the children playing. "All in one nest," he sighed to himself. And now so empty.

10

It was just past two in the afternoon and the sun provided little shade in the east patio of the fort. Graciella and the others had left the site behind Pete Montoya and the ambulance, and were now clustered around the Ft. Burgwin office under the covered *portal* that ran along three sides of the patio. The workers had dispersed and Horace was in his office describing the discovery of the body to Karen Brown.

Ned had encouraged Graciella, who was still pale, to go to her room and rest, but she had refused. She did not want to be alone. She also had not wanted to try to explain the room collapse to Greg, who was obviously anxious to learn more details. The site was now off-limits to inspection by anyone except the police, yet Greg was fearful that more of the structure might fall or, worse, that the forensics people would do some damage.

They had recounted the event from each of their perspectives and now, as the tension began to subside and the initial shock began wearing off, there was little more to say about it. Their faces revealed the stress and fatigue that accompany the aftermath of disaster.

Maria moved to Graciella, putting an arm around her shoulders. "Let's go sit," she coaxed. "I'll brew some tea and we'll try to relax." She turned to Ned and Greg. "Let's give her time to get some color back," she said.

◇◇◇

In the Commander's Quarters, the two of them sat at opposite ends of the sofa, a pot of tea and sandwiches on the coffee table before them. While Maria prepared these in the kitchen, Graciella had sat silently, and few words were exchanged as they each took a sandwich and began eating.

Now, Maria shifted one leg beneath her to face Graciella. "There are some things we must tell each other, Graciella," she said. "Events have now gotten out of hand and we have a murder to explain."

Graciella leaned her head back against the sofa and put her hands up to her temples. The bandage was still there. "Oh, God," she said. She had been saying that a lot, lately. Maria was right. Things were getting out of hand, and Graciella was now convinced that, somehow, she was the cause of it all.

"What's happening to me, Maria?" she asked in a plaintive voice. "I don't know what's real and what is fantasy." She looked over at Maria. "I don't even know who I am," she said, her voice trembling. "What's happening?"

Maria fixed her eyes on Graciella's and held her gaze for a moment. "I wish I could tell you, Graciella," she said. "I do know that you have changed over the past year. Not dramatically, but I have seen subtle changes since you decided to take 'Graciella' as your name." Maria paused, deciding whether to pursue this particular issue now. Perhaps she should approach it. "When you told me about the incident at the site—that breath of cool air which momentarily caught your attention—you passed it off as a curiosity. But I think you were more troubled by it than you admitted."

"I was not alarmed," said Graciella. "I just couldn't explain it. I guess it continued to nag me. Sort of like a memory that keeps coming back." Graciella folded her hands in her lap and looked down at them. "When I took the name," she said, "I didn't connect it with that experience. It was my own decision. It was long after—a month or so—after we backfilled the site."

Maria took the cue. "Tell me, Graciella. Tell me about the name. You told us it had been your name as a child, that you had given it up for 'Grace' when you grew up. That you now decided you would take it back." Maria paused. "There is more to it, isn't there?"

Graciella clasped her hands together, lacing and unlacing her fingers, looking down at them. She inhaled deeply and slowly exhaled. It had been so long ago.

◇◇◇

She was in fourth grade, in Weatherford, Texas. The county seat, Weatherford was a small town of 12,000 on the undefined boundary of the West: cattle, horses, truck farming consumed the lives of most residents. The West Texas cowboy image competed with the growing migration of white collar workers from Fort Worth, attracted to this quiet country thirty miles west on the interstate.

Her father was a banker and they lived in one of the stately Victorian homes with gingerbread trim. She was a popular fourth grader in the small elementary school of 300 students. Mostly White. Mostly friendly. One little girl in her class was Hispanic. Graciella Mendoza. A cute little girl, dark brown skin, an oval face with large brown eyes and pigtails. Very shy. Her parents were tenant farmers on a hay farm outside town. Grace and Graciella played together at recess and sat next to each other in class. Grace had let her hair grow so she could wear pigtails, too.

On her tenth birthday Grace had a fine party at her house. It was October and the afternoon sun sieved through the large pecan tree in her backyard, laying out patterns on the grass and picnic tables. The children had teamed up for one-legged sack races, and Grace was teamed with Billy Sullivan. Grace secretly liked Billy, in the way ten-year-olds identify boy-girl relationships on the eve of discovering sexuality. She and another girl shyly and awkwardly competed for Billy's attention, and the other girl had gained most of it this school-year. Which was why Grace had planned to race with him. They hopped and fell twice, laughing, and won the race. Then Billy had said, "You should play more with us sometimes. Why do you spend so much time with Graciella?"

"I like her," Grace had said, laughing. "What's wrong with that?"

"She's only a Mexican," Billy had replied. "She should play with her own."

Grace had been angry at this, but forgot about the remark as she and Billy continued to play, and she sat next to him for ice cream and cake.

On Monday at recess Billy had come to get Grace to play kickball with him and another boy. Grace and Graciella had been swinging. "Graciella, you come, too," Grace had said.

"No, Grace, just you," Billy had said. He flicked her pigtails. "You're around her so much you're beginning to look like her." He laughed and he and Grace went off to play. Several times Grace looked back to see Graciella swinging alone.

The next day Grace played mostly with Billy and his friends, and said little to Graciella, who again played alone. Grace thought about this that evening and discussed it briefly with her father and mother. They all agreed that Grace had been wrong to ignore Graciella; that she had probably hurt her feelings. Tomorrow, Grace agreed, she would apologize to Graciella.

On Wednesday Graciella had been absent. And thereafter. Her family had moved to another farm near Aledo. That night Grace didn't eat dinner. She lay in her bed and cried. She never saw Graciella again.

◇◇◇

"Graciella, are you all right?" Maria stood before her with a tissue. Tears streamed down her face, dripping onto her hands, which Graciella had tightened into fists. She took the tissue and dabbed her face.

"I'm sorry, Maria," she sniffed. "I'm okay. What was I saying?"

"I had asked you about your name," Maria said. "If you don't want to talk right now, that's okay." She sat again.

"No, Maria," Graciella looked at her. "I should tell you." She reached for the cup and took a sip of tea. "I have. . . visions. . .like daydreams," Graciella looked at her, ". . .but they're so real! I believe, somehow, they <u>are</u> real."

"Visions," Maria said. "You mean like a trance?"

"Yes," said Graciella. "I guess. They only happen occasionally—I've had three—the last one was this morning."

"How long have you had these?" Maria asked.

"The first one was after the incident at the site last year. A month or so after," Graciella said. "It's when I took my name."

"Can you tell me about it?" Maria looked at her intensely.

"Yes. I had been over to the site, checking the bearing of the excavation marker from the benchmark—you know, the iron rebar in cement that serves as our reference in mapping." Graciella held the tea cup on her lap, rotating it back and forth with both hands. "I had taken the readings and was sitting in my Explorer writing them down. I was suddenly aware of a scent of juniper, very strong, carried on a cool, light breeze. Then sagebrush. I didn't fall asleep—I was aware of everything. But the scene sort of shimmered and changed. I was a young girl, about ten, and I was in the pueblo. Pot Creek pueblo." She took another sip of tea.

"But it was back then, in the past, when it was occupied," Grace looked at her. "It was the same site, Maria, the same hills, but there were people living there. I could smell corn roasting. I could see smoke rising from hearths. I could hear children playing in the plaza where I stood,"

. . .and their laughter filled the plaza as it echoed off the houses,
and they danced a rhythm beaten by a child on earthen drum.

A little girl, all painted on the face in black and yellow,
now leaves the circling dancers and approaches. . .smiling, asks me. . .
"'What's your name?'

"'I have no name', I answer, and, although alert, I have no doubt at all that this is true: I have no name."

You have a name, we know your name. She dances back into the circle.
Say your name and you can dance, and we will practice like the elders,
say your name and you will join us. . .not be left to watch with sadness.

"And then I knew, as if I had known but had long before forgotten, and in the strengthening rhythm of the drumbeats, someone spoke it: 'Graciella'!"

Graciella! Graciella! They repeat it all together,
and in tempo with their dancing: Graciella!. . .and it ceases.
Silence now, as in the echo of the final drumbeat, standing, they
appraise me. . . these small children. What's your clan name, Graciella?
Then from somewhere back behind me comes a kiva elder, smiling.
She is Turtle People, children, says the elder gently chiding.
But you knew this. . . Graciella, come and help your anpaíuna;
she is grinding. . . .

"I went with him towards the houses; I remember clearly the *koye*—the grinding room—the manos and metates. Then it was over, and I just sat there for awhile trying to figure it out."

Graciella sat still, came out of her reverie, turned to Maria. "That room, Maria, is the one excavated in Unit III many years ago. It had adobe mealing bins all lined up near one wall. Metates fit into them and the women would lean against the wall and grind corn, pushing the meal down off the metate into the bin, onto a piece of deer skin."

"And in that vision you became Graciella," Maria said.

"I became Graciella. I am Graciella. From that point, Maria, I had <u>always</u> been Graciella—as if never using any other name. Since then, the name 'Grace' has an alien ring to it."

They sat in silence for awhile. Maria got up, went to the kitchen, put more hot water and tea in the pot, and brought it back. She sat again, thinking. "That was no dream," she said finally. "Even as you recounted it, you became someone else. Your voice was changed. They were not your words. There was a cadence." She looked at Graciella.

"Do you have a sister, Graciella?" she asked.

"No," said Graciella. "I'm an only child."

"The word you used, *anpaíuna*. It means 'younger sister'."

"I know," said Graciella.

She pressed the bridge of her nose, massaging it. She always remembered everything, and understood. Even the Tiwa language.

"Do you believe it was real, Maria?" she asked. "I mean, more than some vivid imagining, more than some fantasy?"

Maria looked at her, knitting her brow, her hand absently toying with a strand of hair. "If you mean <u>really</u> real, some reality that exists outside your own psyche, I honestly can't think so," said Maria, cautiously. "But these journeys you take are real enough for you, and that's what matters."

"No," said Graciella, "what matters is what is <u>really</u> real." She turned to Maria, reached up, and removed the dressing on her temple. "Look, Maria," she said. "Tell me what you see."

Maria looked. She stood, came over to Graciella's end of the sofa, and turned on the lamp. She looked closely. "There's nothing there," she said in surprise. "Not even a mark!"

"And here," said Graciella, removing the others. "Look!"

Maria stood dumfounded. "Graciella, I brought you to the hospital. You had real abrasions. Your elbow had a nasty cut! How did these disappear?"

"My Aztec brothers," Graciella said. "In my most recent journey, this morning. They healed me. Do you know my Aztec name, Maria?"

"Your Aztec. . ."

"It's *Huetxochitl*," Graciella said. "It means 'Smiling Flower'. It was my first clan name."

Maria sat down, staring at Graciella in amazement.

"This is <u>really</u> real, Maria; believe it!" Graciella said. "I need you to have no doubts. I can't handle <u>today</u>, this evening, this separate reality, by myself! You can't help me understand what's happening unless you <u>know</u> this."

Maria said nothing, staring at Graciella as in shock. Something in Graciella, some inner messenger within yet beyond her, quietly urged her towards a conclusion. A closure between there and here, then and now. She reached over and took Maria's hand, holding it tightly.

"What's my name?" she asked.

"It's Graciella," Maria replied.

"No, Maria, my <u>last</u> name," Graciella pressed. "What's my last name?"

"It's. . .it's. . ." Maria started, then looked at her quizzically.

"Come on, Maria!" Graciella insisted. "You know me! I'm Grace, I'm Graciella. . .*what is my last name?*"

Maria furrowed her brow, looking into Graciella's eyes. She searched there for the answer. The name! What is it? She stammered, "It's. . .your name is. . .." She slowly shook her head. "I. . .I have forgotten!" She laughed nervously. "How silly is this!" she exclaimed. "I. . .just. . .don't. . .know!"

Graciella patted Maria's hand, trying to smile, not succeeding. "Of course you don't," she said softly. "I'm no longer a last name." She stood. "God help me, I'm mixed in with powers I don't understand and ought to fear, but don't." She turned at the door. "And after I leave, you'll probably remember."

11

What was her name, again? *Grace Underwood*, Ben Sandoval read from the typed report Pete Montoya had given him, *b. 10/12/72; Weatherford, TX; grad. Std. at SMU, Dallas; anthropology. Living at F.B. since June; planning return TX Sept. Excavating kiva, Pot Creek ruins. Injured 8/23 at site when floor, wall collapsed. M. Stern took Holy Cross hospital. Released mid-pm. Brought to F.B. by M. Stern and G. Parson. Stayed in qtrs, slept. Came to site about 9 am. G. Parson removed brush, found body.*

Ben re-read his own notes from the interview. Maria Stern had referred to her as 'Graciella'. Her real name? No, Ben recalled. Pete had not asked her, but had taken her name from the registration tag on the Explorer's visor.

He looked at his watch. Seven o'clock. He had stopped at Holy Cross after leaving the pueblo, then gone to his office, got Pete's notes and a photo of the deceased taken at the scene, and returned to Fort Burgwin. There he had interviewed those not at the ruin earlier: Felix Mondragon, workers in the kitchen, two students, Danny Sheffield and Andrea Abbott; and the secretary, Karen Brown, who had left the site before he had talked to her.

Felix had been repairing a bridge rail near one of the student casitas and had not heard the sirens, while his two workers, in the pickup to fetch more lumber, had followed the sirens to the site. Sheffield and Abbott had been off-site working at the time. All had reasonable—probably defensible—alibis at the estimated time of the murder. Karen Brown, too. She, Sheffield and Abbott occupied both floors of the chalet across the highway from the fort, just down from the site, but she had been in the office working.

Karen Brown was the only one of these who recognized the victim. That was strange, he thought, as he looked again at his notes. Karen had seen Grace and Felix talking at the tool storage room two mornings ago—the day before Grace's accident. Grace had left, Brown recalled, and shortly after that Anita

Lujan had emerged from the office across the patio and had left. No, Karen had not remembered seeing her before, which is why she watched her long enough to later recognize her from the photo.

Had Felix left before Anita did? Karen wasn't sure, but thought he was still in the tool room at the time. Felix had not recognized the photo image, was a bit reluctant to examine it closely. Understandable, Ben thought.

At five-thirty he had received an urgent call from Pete Montoya. He was calling from his police cruiser. They had found Anita Lujan's automobile, a red Honda two-door. Across Highway 518 at the Forest Service's Pot Creek Cultural Site. Ben met Pete there.

The Cultural Site was a mile-long nature trail and a restored small pueblo room with kiva. On the same side of the highway as Pot Creek Pueblo, it was scarcely a quarter-mile north of the fort, but a far shorter distance through pinyon-juniper scrub from the Pot Creek excavations. The Cultural Site was just inside the Carson National Forest boundary. The small ruin had been excavated and restored several years earlier by volunteers from the Forest Service, Taos Archeological Society, and Indians from both Taos and Picuris Pueblos. Indian volunteers and Service personnel took turns hosting visitors during the day. A Forest Ranger discovered the vehicle when he went to close the site at 4:30 pm. He had called the police department.

The Honda had been unlocked, with keys in the ignition and Anita's purse on the passenger-side floor. "Damndest thing," said Pete when Ben arrived. "She must have been trusting, or in a hurry. Looks like nothing's disturbed. But we didn't touch it, Ben."

Ben had called forensics immediately. When they arrived he cautioned them to check every detail, including dirt on the tires and vacuumed debris from the floor. Then he had returned here, to the office.

He sent out for pizza and settled down with his notes, which he was now reviewing for the fifth or sixth time. The autopsy report had come in while he was out. It corroborated what the M.E. had predicted. Death from a thin, sharp object—double-edged—thrust between the ribs, knicking the fifth rib. Punctured the heart. Probably a large knife. Could have been held in either hand. Could have been wielded by an adult male or female. Death was almost instantaneous, with little pain. Thank God for that, Ben said to himself. He would tell Tony. Time of death was between two-thirty and four p.m.

Ben checked his notes again. Grace had been released at 3:30, and probably the three of them arrived at the fort at, say, 3:45. Anita was in Grace's hospital room no later than 3:00. The husband of the woman in the bed next to Grace remembered Anita, thinking it must have been around 2:30. Greg and Maria had been in her room at 3:00 or just before, and the doctor had visited at 3:10—fortunately noting the time on her chart.

Ben whistled to himself. That cuts it close, he thought. Anita must have driven to Pot Creek immediately after leaving Holy Cross. Was the murder committed while Grace and the others were still on the Pot Creek highway? New Mexico 518 curves a lot though the valley, Ben thought. Perhaps they had seen the murderer pass them, without knowing. Only if the murderer had driven north towards them, instead of south over U.S. Hill to Peñasco, he said to himself. If the murderer had driven anywhere: he would not yet rule out someone at the fort.

Ben took a pad of lined paper and placed it before him. With a pencil he drew a vertical line down the middle. On the left, at the top, he wrote "Motive" and underlined it. On the right, he wrote "Opportunity". He poised his pencil under the first word. What was the motive for Anita's murder? Most murders are personal: quarrels over money, infidelity, insult; and most murderers know their victims: a boyfriend, a co-worker, a relative. He wrote these down, with question marks beside each.

No, he scratched them out. Consider the circumstances: Anita's murder is tied to the location, he said to himself. Would she have died had she not gone to Pot Creek? He thought not. Was it a random act, a murder of opportunity? Did someone happen upon her by accident? Kill her to take something? Also not likely, Ben thought; she had no possessions with her. Her purse, money. . .what else?. . .were in her unlocked car. Keys in the ignition.

Turn it around: did she happen upon someone there? Someone who didn't want others to know? Was she witness to another crime?

But what crime? There was nothing at the site to steal, was there? He made a note: "Check with Parson and Underwood at site—anything missing or disturbed?"

No, he said to himself, I'm on the wrong track here. The key must lie with Anita herself. She went there hurriedly. For a purpose. "Discover her purpose," he wrote, "and discover the motive." Why had she been in a hurry? She had left from the hospital, immediately after speaking to Grace. What had she told her? He looked through his notes and found it: something about Grace being where she shouldn't have been when she had the accident. Perhaps Anita decided at that point to go to Pot Creek. Why? He wrote: "Why was Anita at Holy Cross? Because Grace was there? How did she know?"

Ben moved to the "Opportunity" column. He checked his notes for each name. Assuming the murder occurred while Grace, Maria and Greg were on their way to the fort, that certainly let them out. It could have happened afterwards, he thought, but one of them would have had to drive immediately to the site upon arriving. Yet they had all gone to Grace's room. The three of them had good alibis.

Who was at the fort when they arrived? His notes indicated that Felix Mondragon, Horace Stern, and Ned Aberle had met them at Grace's apartment. They had been at the fort during the entire afternoon. He wrote down their names.

Felix Mondragon—he and two workers had been repairing the bridge all afternoon. They each had alibis for the other two. Alberto Sanistevan and Luis Garza were their names. They were very nervous about Grace excavating at the site. Felix had confirmed that they were superstitious, believing that evil spirits were associated with it. Were they afraid of some evil Grace might release there? Possibly, Ben thought. Angered, too? Enough to want to stop Grace, or anyone else? Doubtful. He made a note to check their stories more carefully. Felix had been very concerned about Grace, but apparently shared none of the superstition. He had taken the backhoe to her. "It's a miracle that wall didn't crush her," he had said, "or drive her pick into her when it fell. I should have been there with her."

Horace Stern—he had been in the Geology Lab talking to Ned when the secretary had transferred the call from Maria at Holy Cross. He had been in the office when Greg had arrived from Albuquerque—12:15, according to his notes—and Greg had driven to the hospital immediately. Horace had then gone to his quarters for lunch while Karen had eaten in the office. Between 1:30 and the time Grace and the others returned to the fort at 3:45 or so, Horace had been in and out of the office. Karen had taken Maria's call at 3:30, notifying them that they were on their way back. Karen had a strong alibi—she could not have risked leaving the office, even when Horace was out. Horace, however, had had the opportunity. Ben made another note.

Ned Aberle—he had been in his lab when Grace was taken to the hospital. After the call from Maria, he had volunteered to go to the site, retrieve Grace's equipment, and drive her Explorer back. He had returned to the office after lunch to inquire about Grace, then had gone back to the geology lab to work. Alone. His time was unaccounted for until Grace and the others returned. Ben made a final note.

The two archeology students, Danny Sheffield and Andrea Abbott, had solid alibis: Andrea was with the state crew at Peñasco all afternoon, and Danny had been in Miranda Canyon with the Forest Service archeologist. Both had returned to the fort close to five o'clock. The two art students who had been at the scene after the ambulance had arrived had been in Taos together all afternoon.

Finally, the kitchen crew had all arrived about 2 p.m. to prepare dinner. None had left the building before dinner.

Ben sat back and looked at the "Opportunities" column. Horace and Ned had to be suspects, he thought, at least because they alone had opportunities. Also Felix, Alberto and Luis. Five people. But where was the motive?

"Ben," Pete Montoya stuck his head in the door. "The forensic guys are finished. The Honda has been towed and they left it outside."

Ben looked up. "Thanks, Pete," he said. "Ask Collins to bring me the report when he's finished. Anything important?"

"They didn't find nothing unusual, far as I know."

Ben thought for a moment. "I want to see the contents." He got up and followed Pete into the property room. Pete pointed to a large plastic bag on the table. It was tagged. "It's all yours, amigo," he said.

Ben emptied the bag on the table and sifted through it. One earring, several coins, some kleenex, miscellaneous ticket stubs and other paper fragments comprised the small items. Also a pair of high-heeled black shoes, a wide cowhide belt, a blouse on a hanger, and a box of audio tapes. He examined each item as he replaced it in the bag. As he secured the bag, he noticed a smaller one next to it. He read the tag. It was vacuumed debris from the car's floor. He spread a large sheet of heavy white paper on the table, then emptied the bag onto it. He used his finger to spread the material out. It was mostly dust motes and dirt. One postage stamp. Couple of paper clips. And two small feathers.

He stared at the feathers. Each was about two inches long, an inch and a half wide. Gray. Toward the end of each quill it was mostly down. Down feathers.

Ben left the room and found Pete, preparing to leave. "Pete," he asked, "is Collins still here?" Frank Collins was the forensic man in Taos. Trained in Tucson and, later, Phoenix, he was meticulous in his work and very fussy about anyone interfering with a scene before he got there. He had been the man who followed Ben to the site earlier. He had spent two hours in the hot depression where the victim was found. He had been grateful that the site had been spared the afternoon rain.

"Yeah, I think so, Ben," Pete said. "I'm heading home, okay?"

"See you tomorrow, Pete," Ben said. He walked down the hall, where a light shone from Collins' combination office/laboratory.

Collins was at a small table, writing his report. He had refused to use a computer, and the secretaries had mildly resented having to re-type his longhand reports. He looked up as Ben knocked lightly on the door frame.

"Detective Sandoval," he said. "Come in. I'm just finishing my inventory from the Honda." The inventory was a list of bags, envelopes, and other containers holding the items taken from the car. The contents would be carefully examined and analyzed tomorrow. "I trust you don't need any analyses done before morning."

"Not at all," Ben said. "Frank, when you examined the site today, did you happen to find any of these?" Ben held up one of the feathers.

"What is it," Frank removed his glasses, "a feather?"

"A turkey feather, Frank."

Frank didn't ask if it were important; everything was important to Ben Sandoval—which is why Frank enjoyed working with him. Both were professionals. Frank replaced his glasses and reached for a folder on the table, opened it, ran his finger down a list. "No," he said. "No feathers, Ben." He reached for the feather in Ben's hand. "Why is it important?"

"This one came from the car of the victim," Ben said. "Two of them. They're used in pueblo ceremonies."

Frank returned the feather. "Then you may be interested in this," he said, reaching behind him and retrieving a small pouch from the counter next to a microscope. He held it out for Ben.

"Where did you find it?" Ben asked, examining it. It was a small deerskin pouch with rawhide drawstrings.

"I didn't," Frank replied. "The M.E. found it in a pocket of the victim's uniform. Brought it over with his report. I plan to give the contents a microscopic exam tomorrow."

"No need, Frank," Ben said. He moved over to Frank, held the pouch under the light, and opened it. He put finger and thumb in and extracted a pinch of yellow granules.

Frank smiled. "And, of course, you're going to tell me what this is," he said.

"Corn pollen, Frank," Ben said. "Also used in ceremonies."

He tossed the pouch on the table. "I'm going back to Pot Creek tomorrow morning."

"To find a feather?"

"To find a feather. She would not have carried the one without the other. Feather and pollen." He left with the feather and replaced it and the other debris in the small plastic bag. Then he turned off his desk light and left.

It was starting to become clearer, now, Ben thought. Ritual. He expected, tomorrow, to find more than a feather.

He expected to find a motive.

12

Antonio Romero urged his horse over the last rise before the descent to Blue Lake—*Pawe'ata*. The trail was well-beaten by now, over eighty people having passed along it earlier today. He encountered, here and there, small puffs of white turkey down tied to bushes and tree limbs along the way. The ceremonial marking of sacred ground. The forest of spruce and fir pressed close as he climbed, punctuated with an occasional clearing where ancient glacial ice had left rock debris as the small glacier had receded.

It was four-thirty and the late afternoon sun had already thrown deep shadows across the south face of *Maw'aluna* before the trail had turned along its east face twenty minutes ago. On his right, in the distance, Tony could see an adjacent mountain face still in sunlight. This would be Bow Mountain—*W'ilpianta*—and near its timberline a large stand of aspen shimmered as their leaves reflected their pale green colors. The peak of Taos Mountain continued up to Tony's left, now, and as he reached the edge of the valley of Blue Lake almost everything was in shadow. The sound of chanting voices, to a single drum, filled the valley and flowed over its rim.

The lake lay below him, its frigid water darkened by the stream-fed humus of the surrounding forest soil. Tall white fir and blue spruce, and a few Engleman spruce, dominated the high mountain forest. They rose closely together on the distant side, descending almost to the lakeshore, only the tallest of them still catching the sun. On the near side were numerous clearings where log and brush shelters stood, the fires before them sending narrow columns of smoke directly skyward, like pillars supporting an invisible roof.

At the eastern lakeside, a kiva chief in ceremonial costume sat addressing the young boys who were to be initiated. They formed a half-circle around him, facing the water, wearing only kirtles or breech-cloths. They were learning and memorizing, listening and repeating, in the oral tradition of the ancients. The vehicle for passing yesterday into tomorrow. The only vehicle for wisdom—until the Spanish, and the Mexicans, and the U.S. Congress had brought their faster and coarser vehicles of written texts and treaties and laws, to be all too casually obeyed or not. Tony reflected on past arguments with the Taos school to allow boys and girls to participate in ceremonies such as this—to miss classes for so trivial a reason as to learn the meaning of "being Indian", and of "community". For which there were no textbooks.

He held his horse for a moment and reflected on the scene below, a solemn and contented scene too soon to be irreparably damaged. Then he moved slowly down to the lake.

◇◇◇

At eight o'clock the next morning, Ben Sandoval received a call from the Pueblo. "Bring her home to us, Ben," Tony said.

◇◇◇

As Ben was taking his call, Graciella was finishing breakfast in the dining hall. Greg joined her with his tray. "Grace, I hope you're feeling better this morning," he said as he sat. "I'll tell you I didn't sleep very well."

"Me, too, Greg," she said. "Thanks. I'm almost as good as new." She took a sip of coffee. "I'm sorry we couldn't talk yesterday. I'll be glad to tell you anything now."

Greg frowned. "It just seems so impossible, Grace. First, your accident—so implausible that the structure should fall—and then the murder." He began eating.

"I don't want to talk about the murder," she shivered slightly. "That poor girl!"

"But the site," said Greg. "Can you think of <u>anything</u> that might explain it?"

"I've been thinking about that, Greg," she said. "I've got a thought." She paused. "Now, this is really off the wall, okay?"

Greg smiled. "Grace, you know that most sound explanations begin as off-the-wall ideas."

"Let me get more coffee," she said. She returned her tray to the kitchen pass-through and refilled her coffee. "Okay," she said, sitting again. She put her elbows on the table and folded her hands in front of her. "Suppose the kiva was built in what was the plaza, but very close to the room block. It continued being used as the room block expanded around it on all sides except south. So it was still a plaza kiva. Suppose, then, something happened and they decided to build <u>over</u> the kiva, expanding the room block—not <u>around</u> it, but on top of it."

Greg gave her a look of skepticism. She paused to take a sip of coffee. "But they didn't want to abandon the kiva. It was important for some ceremony, say, or was particularly sacred. So they wanted to continue using it. They simply changed the kiva roof to make it level with the gound, reinforced it with extra vigas, and put some rooms on top of it. They didn't fill it in because they used it, entering from a room rather than from the plaza."

She took another sip and held the cup. "Then, when they abandoned the pueblo, the kiva lay hidden and protected beneath the surface rooms—sealed even from fire. When the structure finally began collapsing, the heavy kiva vigas continued to support the weight above. When we began excavating that part of Unit VII, we removed a ton of overburden that had become stabilized over the centuries. We shifted a delicate balance. The rotting roof timbers of the kiva finally released stresses in one direction and received new stresses in another."

She took a deep breath. "And so the collapse began," she finished. "Slowly, after we excavated last year and then backfilled; more rapidly, when I re-excavated; then, my strike with the pick was the final, small stress needed, and it collapsed entirely."

Greg looked at her. "Like a house of cards," he said. "Or the harmonic vibration of a battalion of footsteps marching across a bridge." He sat thinking as he ate. "Interesting."

"Well," she said, "what do you think?"

"Grace, aside from the archeological problems, it makes some sense," said Greg. "Let's look at what it explains: first, it explains the collapse <u>after</u> your excavation; second, it explains why there was no depression in that part of the site <u>before</u> our initial excavations last year. Third, it explains the GPR readings we got."

Greg thought some more. "What it doesn't explain is why there was no hint of settling when we removed the heavy overburden in the initial excavation," he said. "Despite the fact that within a month that excavation was backfilled, there were all those weeks with the weight removed. Why didn't it begin to sag then?"

"I think I can answer that," said Graciella, developing the thought as she spoke. "It wasn't the shift in weight alone that set this thing in motion," she said. "It was that plus seepage which invaded the dry and sealed kiva." Her voice rose slightly in pitch as this insight came to her. "Greg, you'll remember the cool air I felt during the final cleaning of Room 703 last year. We had exposed the underground chamber to air through the posthole!" She became excited now. "The afternoon rains that year! Although we covered the site each day, water seeped into it," she concluded, "and down into the roof timbers of the kiva. A year of slow rotting has passed since then, creating instability now where there was none before!"

"Damn!" said Greg after a moment. "That would explain it, Grace. Logically, it certainly could have happened that way."

Graciella looked at him, smiling. "Okay," she said. "What are the archeological problems you mentioned?"

Greg smiled back at her. "You know what they are! There's absolutely no precedent for this, architecturally," he said. "There are central 'big' kivas, there are kivas in plazas associated with room clusters, and in some places like Acoma and a few prehistoric sites on the Rio Grande, there are in-room kivas: kivas incorporated into surface units as rooms." He shook his head, "but there are no below-room kivas. Not here, not anywhere in the Southwest. How would you explain an absolutely unique anomaly found only at this site?"

Graciella frowned. "I can't explain it, Greg. But," she pointed at him, "the basin and center-post are also absolutely unique here." She paused, finishing her coffee. "Greg, the Northern Tiwa are unique in many ways, archeologically and ethnographically. Isolated language. No masked kachina dances. No clan organization. Apache and Commanche influences found nowhere else. This was a cultural fringe. An outlier. That's where innovation and variation abound!" She taunted him, "Remember the center-edge hypothesis? You taught it to me! At the edge of an ecosystem you get strangeness." She laughed. "And at the edge of the pueblo world you get Pot Creek!"

Greg laughed with her, shaking his head. "*Touché*," he said. "I sit humbled and reminded of my own teaching. But," he pointed back at her, "the proof is in the excavation. When the investigators release the site, you and I are going to test your 'underground kiva' hypothesis."

Horace and Maria had come through the line and approached their table.

"May we join you two?" asked Horace. "Good morning," Greg replied, moving his tray. "Please do."

"Graciella, you're looking much better this morning," said Maria. "I see you put on fresh bandages."

Graciella looked at Maria inquisitively, but got only an innocent smile. "Yes, Maria," she smiled back. "I took a shower and decided to replace the dressings. The wounds are almost healed already." Graciella had improvised new dressings, not wishing to answer embarrassing questions, which were sure to come if she had not worn some covering.

"That's very good to hear, my dear," Horace smiled benevolently. "But I want you to be especially careful for a few days. A concussion is not a trivial thing." He looked at Greg. "By the way, Lieutenant Sandoval called a short while ago. He's coming back out this morning. Wants to visit the site again."

"Yes?" said Greg. "I hope he'll release it soon. Grace and I have to test a hypothesis. When's he coming? I want to talk to him."

"So does he, Greg," Horace said. He looked at Graciella. "He wants to talk to you both. Asked if you would be available."

"Actually," Maria interrupted, "he wants to talk to all of us, even Felix and his workers."

"Actually, Love," Horace said to her, "he simply asked that everyone be available—except for Sheffield and Abbott, who have an early schedule. I had the impression he's going to the site first."

◇◇◇

Ben Sandoval had removed the dried chamisa that had blown into the depression. He stepped gingerly over several of the fallen wall fragments and carefully knelt down to examine the space between and below them. Some of the lower fragments had wedged together, protecting some chamber below into which Ben could reach but not probe. He withdrew his arm and began examining the surrounding debris. Nothing.

"Lieutenant, good morning," Greg said from atop the mound. He had stepped over the police tape marking the spot as a crime scene, and peered down at Ben.

"Dr. Parson," Ben said, squinting up at him through the morning sun. He reached up, "Give me a hand." Greg took Ben's hand and arm and helped him out. "Thanks," Ben said, dusting himself off. He wore a western shirt patterned in small black and white checks, blue jeans, and boots. "A little delicate down there," he said. "You know there's an open pit down below? Feels like it could collapse further."

"It's what I'm worried about," Greg said. "I really need you to release your restrictions so we can get the debris out and stabilize the site."

"You got it, Doctor," said Ben. The two of them walked back down the mound to their vehicles. "I'll double check with forensics. One condition: I want to be here when you start digging."

"Fine," said Greg. "What are you looking for?"

"Not sure," Ben said. "But if I find it, I'll know." He leaned against the tailgate of his pickup. "You going to let this student, Grace, continue with the excavations?"

"She and I both will do it," Greg said. "This is a highly unusual phenomenon here. There's no precedent for it. We need to continue as soon as we can, before there's any more collapse."

"Obviously dangerous," Ben said casually. "Is it standard to let students excavate alone?"

"No," said Greg, "and I'm sorry now I let her. Won't happen again."

Greg seemed a bit touchy on the subject. Ben decided to pursue it. "Well," Ben said, "you obviously couldn't have known. Why was she doing this?"

"It's part of her dissertation research," Greg said. "The transition from pithouse to kiva. She excavated the rooms up there last year," he gestured towards Unit VII. "She wanted to excavate the kiva below them this season, but we changed plans." Greg shifted self-consciously. "So I gave her permission to excavate after the close of the season. For one week."

"How did you know there was a kiva below the rooms?" Ben asked.

"GPR," Greg replied. "Gound Penetrating Radar. We did a radar scan before excavations began, got a circular anomaly below Rooms 703 and 704. Strongest echo you'd want. Couldn't have been anything else."

Ben nodded. "Impressive," he said. "Amazing that radar can do that. So you figured she could excavate this kiva in a single week?"

Greg looked at him. "Not the entire kiva," he said. "But she could excavate enough to give us a diameter and a depth. That's part of her research design."

Ben expressed genuine interest. "How so?" he asked.

"Well," Greg said, "she's testing the hypothesis that when pithouses became transformed into kivas, they remained the same, architecturally, for awhile, and held to the same shape and diameter, but they became more shallow."

"Why is that?" Ben wanted to know. He could see Greg's interest rising, and he wanted that.

"Because," Greg explained, "As a pithouse, its use as a residence for a family required depth for insulation and smoke dispersion. As a ceremonial kiva, its size would remain the same or even increase, but depth is no longer critical: it's no longer a home."

"Interesting," Ben said. "So is this Grace's last excavation before she writes the dissertation?"

"This is the last," said Greg.

"How important is it for her research?" Ben asked.

"What do you mean?" Greg raised his eyebrows. Where is he going with this? he asked himself.

"I mean," Ben said, "what would happen if she couldn't finish this last excavation? Would she still have a dissertation?"

"Absolutely," Greg said. "This excavation was something she wanted, personally." He smiled. "It certainly isn't critical, in any way, to completing her degree."

"But she stayed after the regular season to do it," Ben commented. "And alone, at that." He looked up at Greg. "With your permission." Almost to himself, but loud enough, he said, "How unusual. She could have been writing the dissertation instead." Greg did not respond.

Ben looked over the mounds to the north. "If I wanted to go directly to the Pot Creek Cultural Site from here," he asked, "what would be the shortest way?"

Greg pointed off to the left. "Over that small mound beyond the depression there," he said. "There are several footpaths, but no trail. When you come to the Forest Service fence, follow it to the left and you'll see the restored ruin."

"Thanks," Ben said. He started down.

"We'd like to start moving this debris and begin excavating again," Greg said. "Will this afternoon be okay?"

"One o'clock," Ben said. "But don't start until I'm here." He waved and headed off down the unit to the north.

Where the mounds ended, the pinyon-juniper began. There was little underbrush and, as Greg had noted, several pathways. One seemed more direct, to the northwest, and also seemed more worn. Ben followed it. The scrub forest was quite uniform, trees all about ten to fifteen feet high, with sunlight striking the needle-cushioned surface underneath in large patches. No one would leave much evidence of passage.

He timed himself. Walking leisurely, it took him six minutes. The restored adobe ruin had two rooms and an underground kiva. A Forest Service ranger was supervising two workers who were renewing the adobe plaster on one wall. "Morning," Ben said as he approached. "I'm Ben Sandoval, Taos Police." He offered his hand.

"John Briggs," the ranger said, shaking hands. "You investigating the murder?"

"Yes," said Ben. They walked over to the ruin. Beside the two men was a wheelbarrow with wet adobe in it. One was on a ladder scooping adobe from a bucket and spreading it with his hand on the wall. "You fellows been working here pretty regularly?"

"Yes, sir," the one mixing adobe in the wheelbarrow said. "Off and on, you know."

"We have several volunteers," Briggs said. "Different ones come and go during the day. Anita would come and help occasionally. Do you have any clues to who did it?"

"Anita Lujan?" Ben asked, surprised. "How about yesterday? Did you see her here?"

"I wasn't here yesterday," Briggs said. "We had a meeting in the Supervisor's office in the morning."

"She was here in the morning," said the man on the ladder. He stepped down, wiping perspiration with a bandana. "I came in from Picuris, on my way to Taos. Her car was here when I stopped by."

"This is Joe Espinosa," Briggs said. "One of our Picuris volunteers."

"Tell me about it, Joe," Ben said.

"Well, I stopped by—must have been around seven-thirty in the morning. The gate was still locked, and Anita's car was parked just outside. That's why I stopped. But I didn't find her."

Ben took out his pad and pencil and began taking notes. "Didn't find her?" he asked.

"I parked beside her car, figured I'd say hello. I was going to come back about nine-thirty, after I delivered some wood I cut for my brother-in-law in Ranchos. If she needed something, I could bring it back for her, I figured." Espinosa gestured towards the ruin. "I walked up here and looked around. She wasn't nowhere. I though maybe she was on the nature trail somewhere, but I didn't look. I had to get into Ranchos, so I left."

"We usually open around nine, nine-thirty," Briggs said. "Yesterday it was about ten-thirty, because of the meeting."

Ben looked at Espinosa. "Did you come back?"

"Yes. I guess it was about ten. The gate was still locked. But she had left." He looked over at the other man. "About ten-thirty, Jorge came with the key to the gate, and we worked until lunch and left."

"That's right," Jorge said. "But she didn't come back."

"Are you sure it was her car, Joe?" Ben asked Espinosa.

"It was her car," he said.

"Who worked here in the afternoon?" Ben asked Briggs.

"Probably no one, yesterday," he said. "None of the Service personnel were here—we all talked about it. We only came back to lock the gate at 4:30. That's when we discovered her car here."

"Ask around, if you will," Ben said. "Talk to your volunteers. Anyone who might have been here." He gave the men his card. "Call me."

He took the same path back to his pickup at Pot Creek Pueblo, walking rapidly this time. Just under three minutes. Probably two minutes for someone running.

Anita had been here twice yesterday, Ben reflected. Early morning and late afternoon. The first time, she had left alive.

13

Graciella turned a page of her field notes and began entering the information on her computer. This was the last page, and it had taken her almost an hour to get this far. Much of it had to come from memory. Since her first day at the site, too much had happened too rapidly for her to be able to follow the normal procedures. She had been accustomed to transcribing her field records every evening. A little over an hour ago, Greg had come to her apartment with the good news that they could resume work at Pot Creek after lunch—sufficient motivation for her to get this transcription done.

She paused after entering the final measurement she had taken on the overnight settling of Room 703. Details of the collapse would have to await more measurements when she and Greg returned to the site. She would not record the emotional and physical trauma of being part of the collapse, but could not avoid thinking again about it.

Maria had heard her scream, she had said. Had driven to the site from the Art Barn, she had said, and pulled her out. Driven her to the hospital. But I had not screamed, Graciella pressed her memory. I heard it, but it wasn't me. Had it been Maria's scream? Was Maria telling the truth, or could she be more directly involved in this?

Graciella had not wanted to pursue this when she and Maria talked yesterday. It had been enough to test Maria's concern to help her. It had been genuine, Graciella told herself. She was certain that Maria now understood that forces beyond the control of either of them were truly involved; that she, Graciella, had been the focus of these for over a year. What she did not know yet was whether Maria had some additional reason for her concern. She had cautioned Graciella about someone not wanting her to excavate. Graciella was hopeful that, since she had taken Maria into her confidence, the favor would be returned. She would seek her out this evening.

A knock on her apartment door brought Graciella out of her reverie. She opened it. "Lieutenant Sandoval," she said. "Come in. Dr. Stern said you would be dropping by."

"Thank you, Miss Underwood," Ben stepped in. "I just wanted to talk with you a bit, if you're feeling better." He took the chair she offered.

"Please, call me Graciella," she said, sitting on the bed. "I'm fine, thanks."

"'Graciella'," he smiled. "A pretty name. You prefer it to 'Grace'?"

"It was my childhood name," she replied. "I've been using it for over a year." She smiled. "I prefer it, but people still call me 'Grace'."

"Including the Texas Department of Motor Vehicles," Ben returned her smile. "It's the name on your registration," he explained when she looked at him quizzically. "Officer Montoya wrote it down."

"Yes," she said. "I'll be changing that when I return to Texas."

"Graciella," Ben said, casually, "I'm just trying to clear up a few bits of information. I hope you can help." He leaned forward and put his elbows on his knees, folding his hands. "It turns out Anita Lujan was at your site yesterday morning. I'm trying to figure out why."

Graciella expressed surprise. "Morning?" she asked. "She couldn't have been! I would have seen her."

"She parked at the Cultural Site. Walked in from the north end," Ben said. "Maybe she was there before you began excavating."

"Impossible," Graciella said. "Lieutenant, I spent the night there. I came back here for a shower and quick breakfast—less than an hour—at six-thirty." She paused, "Unless she came between then and about seven-thirty, I would have seen her."

"Her car was there after seven-thirty," Ben said. "A worker at the Cultural Site saw her car. She wasn't at the restored ruin, though."

"All I can tell you, Lieutenant Sandoval, is that I was back at the site by then," Graciella said. "Why on earth was she there?"

"That's what I need help on," Ben said, smiling. "Curious, isn't it?" He shifted positions, leaning back with an arm over the back of the chair. "Why did you spend the night at the site?" he asked. "I didn't know archeologists were so dedicated."

She laughed, leaning back on the bed with her hands. "You'd be surprised, Lieutenant," she said. "We eat and sleep with our work, here. Literally." Graciella caught the glint of humor in his eyes. "I'll bet you do the same," she said. "Work late, sleep in the office, maybe send out for pizza?"

He laughed. "Don't remind me," he said. "Maybe we're just an unusual pair of dedicated professionals."

"Actually," Graciella became serious, "we've had some vandalism. I didn't want it to happen again."

Ben raised his eyebrows. "Kind of dangerous, being out there all by yourself. Tell me about it."

Graciella recounted the events: the site being filled in mysteriously overnight, her fruitless search for evidence pointing to the culprit, her permission to use the backhoe, Ned bringing her dinner and bedroll after she had re-cleared the excavation. When she had finished she offered Ben coffee and poured cups for them. "So I figured it was a nasty prank," she said, returning to the bed. "Not something that might put me in danger. I was angry. I wasn't going to allow it to happen again."

"It was an uneventful night, I assume?" Ben asked.

"Completely," Graciella said. "I read by the Coleman until ten, then fell asleep. Woke up at 6:30. The site was fine. No prankster." She looked at him. "No Anita Lujan," she said.

"We'll see," said Ben. "I'll be joining you at the site this afternoon."

Graciella leaned forward. "Lieutenant Sandoval," she asked. "Do you think there might be some connection between my excavation and Anita's death?"

Ben looked at her. "Graciella," he asked, "how much do you know about Taos Pueblo rituals?"

She gave him a curious look. "A little," she replied. "I've attended quite a few of their dances. Why?"

"Not ceremonies," he said. "Dances are part of the seasonal round. The deer dance, the turtle dance—these and the others are part of their calendar. They occur at scheduled times. They involve ritual, of course, but I'm talking about special rituals—for healing, for cleansing the spirit, for driving evil away." He reached into his pocket and retrieved a feather. "Turkey feathers like this," he said, "and corn meal, and pollen, and other items; these are used in such rituals." He offered the feather and she took it. "Two of these were found in Anita's car. In her pocket was a small skin pouch. It contained pollen."

Graciella examined the feather with fascination. "Ritual," she said, absently.

"Yes," Ben said. "There is a connection, to answer your question. Anita Lujan was at the excavation for a ritual. She never got the chance to perform it."

Graciella sat holding the feather, staring at it. Ben could see in her eyes a brief vulnerability, and knew that her thoughts were elsewhere. She shields it well, he thought, beneath a veneer of self-assurance. The dark eyes were wide, but not in fright. It was not fear that was driving her. It was some uncertainty. Ben had seen the look before. It had been in the eyes of an old Navajo woman who had lived with her husband in a hogan near the Blanco Trading Post south of Farmington. Her son had been killed in an auto accident on the Apache reservation and Ben had brought his belongings to her. She had summoned a wisdom which lay deep in her past and which comforted her as she sat without emotion. But in her eyes was an uncertainty, as if asking "On whom will this wisdom be bestowed, now?" But there was no fear.

Graciella would have a lot more to tell him about this, Ben thought, but he'd have to pry it out with caution. She was beginning, he realized, to hold a special fascination for him.

He reached out and took the feather, gently. Graciella's eyes followed the feather, then focused on Ben. He got up to leave.

"I'm sorry, Lieutenant," Graciella said. "I was trying to imagine what ritual she could have intended. And why."

"It's 'Ben'," he said. "If I'm to call you Graciella, then you must call me 'Ben'."

"All right, Ben," she smiled, but did not rise. She held up a hand to delay him as a thought came to her. "Wait," she said. "I didn't see her, but I may have heard her. As the wall collapsed on me, I heard a scream. It was the scream that brought Maria; she thought it was me." She looked up. "It wasn't me. Could it have been Anita?"

"It could have been," Ben said. "If so, it raises the question why she didn't run to help you." He thought a moment. "Unless she was screaming at something else." He smiled. "Thanks. You've been very helpful."

At the doorway he paused. "You know, Graciella," he said. "If you let that black hair grow longer and braided it like mine," he touched one of his braids, "you would look very Indian."

She looked up at him. "Yes," she said. "I was told that, once."

◇◇◇

Ben walked out the front of the hallway leading from Graciella's apartment and stood outside. The fort building lay directly ahead at the end of the parade ground. The building to his left should be the geology lab. He walked towards it. He assumed that Ned Aberle would be there. If he wasn't, Ben would look around the fort. He needed to become more familiar with its layout, and where people normally worked.

The lab was open and Ben went in. Long tables were grouped in the middle of the rectangular building, and on them lay miscellaneous aerial photos and U.S. Geological Survey quad maps. Counters along both side walls held various microscopes, and in cabinets above them were shelves of rock and mineral samples. Against the far wall were four drafting tables. Ned was seated at one of them.

Ned turned around as Ben approached. "Good morning, Lieutenant," he said. "How is the investigation going?"

"A little progress, Dr. Aberle," Ben said. "These things go very slowly sometimes. I just have a few questions."

"By all means, Lieutenant," Ned said eagerly. "Really, anything I can do to help, I'll be more than happy to."

Ben looked around. "Nice facilities here. You have this all to yourself?"

Ned laughed. "Well, for the time being," he said. "I've got one graduate student finishing some geological mapping up near Questa. I'll be leaving next week. In the meantime," he swept his arms around, "it's all mine!"

"So no one was in here with you yesterday afternoon," Ben said.

"No," Ned said. "I was alone, trying to finish this map." He turned to the large tracing on the drafting board. It lay over one of the U.S.G.S. maps and was inked with lines and symbols indicating faults, contacts, and other geological phenomena.

Ben examined it. "This is interesting," he said. "Exactly what is your research here?"

Ned leaned over and pointed to features on the map. "This entire western face of the ridge behind us," he traced it with his finger, "is Precambrian, over a billion years old." He moved his finger down. "The eastern face is Mesozoic, mostly Mississippian, under 400 million years. But there are places," he indicated, "where the Precambrian pokes through. I'm mapping these."

"You're doing this alone?" Ben asked.

Ned straightened and smiled. "Oh, no," he said. "I've had several students here this summer. I'm consolidating our several maps to get a good profile of the geological history of this valley." He smiled. "But you're not interested in <u>this</u>, Lieutenant. You're interested in my alibi, right?"

Ben returned the smile. "And in whether you can support anyone else's," he said. "But you saw no one, and I guess no one saw you."

"Sorry, Lieutenant," Ned said. "Not after I brought Grace's vehicle back."

"When you got her vehicle, did you go up on the mound?" Ben asked.

"Oh, yes," Ned replied. "I wanted to see where she had fallen—and recover any loose equipment. But I didn't want to risk falling in myself, so I left everything there."

"Left what?" Ben asked.

"You know," Ned said. "The hand mattock and her trowel. They had fallen down where wall debris was wedged against the floor. I figured they'd be safe for the time being."

"Probably a wise move," Ben said. "It was pretty unstable." He gave Ned a casual glance. "What kind of trowel was it?"

"Didn't Grace get it back?" Ned asked. "It's her only one. Had it forever. It's a Marshalltown." Ned laughed. "I kid her about it. She's sharpened it so often it's half its original width. But she treasures it." Ned mused, "She'll want it back. Probably a good-luck piece. Just like my geologist's hammer. Had it fifteen, twenty years."

"We'll be sure to return it to her," Ben said. "Thanks for your time, Dr. Aberle." They shook hands and Ben walked out.

But first, Ben thought to himself, we'll have to find it. Not at the site, though. Murder weapons usually leave with the murderer.

14

As any demolition expert will readily tell you, removing the debris of a collapsed structure is infinitely more difficult than constructing one. Especially if something underneath must be protected. Greg, Graciella and Ben stood atop Unit VII and looked down into the depression. The backhoe had been brought over, but was not positioned yet.

The floor of Room 703 was broken in two sections across the center basin, lengthwise. Its southern part sloped at about twenty degrees down towards the north, with its southern wall tilting forward, but intact. A gap of six to eight inches separated it from the backfilled surface of the unit, but the wall had sunken vertically some eight inches.

The northern half of the floor was canted down forty degrees, where largely intact fragments of the upper course of the north wall had fallen inward. These fragments, some upside down, were wedged between the tilted floor and the second and third wall courses. The lower wall course was not visible, apparently having dropped vertically. The unexcavated fill against which the north wall had rested before collapse had crumbled somewhat, but had held its position. Rootlets and white mineral deposits from seepage identified the surface where that wall had been.

Greg knelt down and gently pulled back on the separated south wall. "This seems fairly stable," he said. "But it won't be safe with us working down there." He stood. "Grace, bring the backhoe up this side. You can swing the shovel below this wall and we can force the wall to collapse into it." He carefully stepped into the depression, testing his footing on the sloping southern part of the floor. "The wall is still attached to the floor here," he said, "and I think the floor has stabilized." He moved to the east corner and measured from floor to surface with his tape. "It hasn't moved at all since yesterday. I think it's well supported from below. Should be okay." He reached down to the fragments of the north wall, moving them gingerly, but with difficulty. "Too heavy for us to lift," he said. "Too entrenched for the backhoe." He looked up. "We'll rig a block and tackle."

"Greg," Graciella peered down from the surface, "do you see my trowel or pick?"

"No," Greg said, climbing back out. "But we won't be doing any trowel work for awhile."

"Can you use the backhoe without doing further damage?" Ben asked.

"Watch me!" Graciella said. "This is the easy part."

And it was. When she had positioned the tractor and swung the shovel over and then down just off the floor, Greg and Ben, on either side of the shovel, carefully pulled the south wall towards them. The wall cracked and large chunks fell into the shovel. Graciella then cupped the shovel and swung it up and over to the right, where she dumped it. Repeating the process three more times had safely removed almost all of the wall. The remainder Greg and Ben cleared with hand shovels.

The backfilled portion was holding, but to be safe Graciella took out enough of it to leave room for any additional settling. It was now a sloping talus that could easily be negotiated as entry to the excavation. Graciella folded the shovel arm of the backhoe and left it in place.

"Remind me never to question your ability with heavy machinery," said Ben as she joined them.

Moving the fallen north wall was not so easy, but was done without further damaging the collapse. Greg rigged a heavy rope with block and tackle to the backhoe arm, then a rope harness at the end. The three of them maneu- vered the three upper chunks of wall, one at a time, into the harness, lifted these using the double pulley, and guided the harness as Graciella raised the arm up and over the surface. As the third one was being shifted to sling the harness under it, they found Graciella's hand mattock.

The lower chunk, wedged into the crevice, would have to be moved by hand. The chunk blocked an opening into what remained of the kiva below, and after removing it they would determine how to remove the broken floor and remaining north wall courses, and discover exactly what was supporting these.

"Let's take a break, here," Greg said. "I want to take measurements now that most of this is exposed." He smiled at Graciella. "The test of your hypothesis is upon us, Grace."

"What hypothesis is this?" Ben asked, as the three walked to the shade of the junipers where the vehicles were parked. The contrasting temperature reminded them of how hot the afternoon sun had become. While Greg went back to the unit with his clipboard and tape, Graciella explained her theory to Ben. She lay back against a tree as she told him how it all seemed to fit together. He sat back on his heels, listening intently. There was enthusiasm and self-assurance in her voice. She appeared confident and relaxed, absorbed in this adventure, her dirt-streaked face beneath the wide-brimmed hat showing none of the stress Ben had seen earlier.

Ben noticed that the dressing on her head had become loose and reached up. "You're losing your bandage," he said, moving to touch it.

Graciella retreated quickly. "No. . .it's. . ," she began, putting her hand up to cover it. She pressed it to her temple, where it stuck. "Thanks, Ben," she said. "It's almost healed. I probably won't need it by tomorrow." She gave him a slightly embarrassed look, and then smiled. But not before he had noted how close to the surface that stress had been. He felt compassion toward her.

"Okay, folks," Greg said, returning. "Time to get back into the sun again."

Ben and Graciella got up as Greg opened his canteen. "You folks are confirming my own theory," Ben laughed. "The romance of archeology is a myth perpetrated on the young. By the time they realize how hard and dirty it is they're hooked."

"Right," Graciella grinned at him sarcastically. "Same myth they use in detective novels: good hours, intellectual challenge, fresh air, great pay."

The three of them carefully examined the remaining wall fragment. It was easily three feet in length, probably weighed two hundred pounds, wedged tightly. At one end, Greg could pass his arm down through a narrow opening. Up to the shoulder, he still could feel no surface. He whistled. "Pretty deep chamber," he said, looking at Graciella. "Your hypothesis just might be correct."

Graciella pressed the blade of a shovel as far under the fragment as she could, while Ben and Greg lifted at one end. With the shovel's leverage, the fragment moved slightly and Greg kicked a cobble under it to prevent it from settling back down into the crevice.

After several attempts, the end nearest the opening had been raised enough to slip one loop of rope around it. They played out a length of about eight feet. Then, standing on the mound surface, Ben and Greg pulled steadily on the rope as Graciella, down below, continued to lever the chunk with her shovel. Slowly, it was released from its hold in the crevice and began tilting up, towards the west, away from its deepest seat. With a fifteen degree angle, now, Graciella got good leverage with her shovel, and together the three of them raised the fragment end-on and vertical. It was free.

They gathered around the exposed opening. It was about a foot and a half long and tear-shaped, its widest part almost a foot across, where floor and wall separated near the northeast corner of the room. It was pitch black below. Graciella looked up at the sky. It was almost three o'clock, and the late afternoon sun shone brightly, casting Greg's shadow over the opening.

"Greg," she said, "move to the side. The sunlight should pass through here." They all knelt down and looked.

At its angle, the sun cast a small, tear-shaped spot of light on a surface below, about four feet east of the opening. It was the adobe floor of the kiva, and part of the circumference of a stone-lined hearth could be seen. Greg took out his tape measure and cautiously extended it vertically through the opening. When it touched the surface, he called out the reading. "Forty-two inches!" he exclaimed.

They all stood and looked at each other. "Congratulations, Grace," Greg grinned widely. "Your hypothesis has been confirmed!"

Graciella stood mutely above the crevice; for her inner self, the crevice was a virtual abyss. She was transfixed. Yes, it was important for her professional self-image that her hypothesis had been confirmed. Yes, congratulations and all of that. But how insignificant, how absolutely, laughably unimportant such a tedious matter was compared with the issue of her identity, of her personal survival, which she urgently wanted resolved by what lay below.

She had lived for fourteen months in an ambiguous reality—or, rather, in a liminal state where several realities alternatively occupied her current space and time. It had begun here and would receive confirmation or denial here. She had guided her efforts to come to terms with it along this very trajectory. Each mysterious journey had encouraged her to affirm her rightful place in another world. She desperately needed to confront the source of those journeys and connect these worlds. She was convinced beyond debate that she would find the answer here. It lay, she knew, forty-two inches below her feet. She was not afraid of it, and she would wait for the opportunity to explore this abyss. But she was excited at the prospect after so long.

"Hey, Ben!" Pete Montoya called from down below. The three of them stood up and looked down the mound to see a police car parked next to their vehicles. Pete waved at them and approached. At the top, he looked down on the three of them.

"Ben?" Pete asked. "Which filthy face is yours?" he asked, as three sweat-streaked faces pretty much pancaked with dirt looked up. Ben raised a hand.

"Jesus Christ, Ben," Pete said. "What the hell you doin', amigo? Look like a Goddamn chain-gang-Charlie!"

"Don't insult us archeologists, Pete," Ben laughed, climbing out of the depression. "What brings you this close to work?"

Pete lowered his voice. "'Tonio Romero called from the Pueblo," he said. "Anita Lujan's brothers, they want to come out here." He whispered, "'Tonio says it's important. Some ritual so Anita's spirit can pass over."

"You call Tony," said Ben, putting his hand on Pete's shoulder. "Have them patch it through from your car radio. Tell Tony it's okay. Whenever they want to. Just let me know."

Pete went to his patrol car while Ben returned to the excavation. Graciella and Greg had chipped away at the floor near the narrower part of the opening and had enlarged it. The suspension of dust had illuminated more of the interior near the top surface. Midway the length of the crevice they could see what broke the collapse and held it stable: a roof timber, shifted from its vertical kiva post on the north side, had collapsed. Still in its proper place on the south side upright, its northern end had fallen and was lodged against a low adobe bench that circled the kiva. Smaller vigas, *latillas*, running across at right angles had fallen in places, but the main bearing viga on the north end, running east to west, had held. The southern and eastern beams, or vigas, were intact.

What was preserved, Greg realized as he cast a flashlight beam inside, was a relatively intact late Thirteenth Century kiva. Maybe early Fourteenth. Astounding, he thought.

"Let me go inside, Greg," Graciella said. "Just briefly, to check the structural integrity."

"You'll wear a rope," Greg said.

They fashioned it into a harness and put it around Graciella's waist and shoulders. She could barely fit into the opening as they lowered her. On the floor inside, she took the flashlight Greg handed her.

"Look very carefully before you take any steps," called Ben. "Better just to stand still and inspect the supports."

Greg nodded in agreement. "We'll want photos from your vantage," he said, "as pristine as possible." He went to get the camera.

Graciella crouched down and swept the flash slowly across the ceiling. Only the northwestern perimeter of the kiva roof had collapsed, she realized, and this was the portion under Rooms 703 and a portion of 704. With her tape she estimated the diameter to be just under 17 feet, with an average height at the perimeter walls of about eight feet. Almost a regular circle, she noted; not "D"-shaped or a flattened east side, as some were.

The roof was cribbed, supported by six vertical posts, each originally about a foot in diameter. The two nearest the excavated rooms above had deteriorated somewhat, and it was from the north-most upright that the roof-supporting north-south viga had slipped, allowing the floor and wall above to sink.

Following the roof beams, Graciella saw a central square—below an unexcavated room just east of 704—cribbed with four-inch vigas and supporting a tool-pecked slab of tabular sandstone. This must have been the roof-hatch, she surmised; through the floor of what would be Room 705.

She moved the flash down directly beneath it. Ladder holes between the ash pit and the east-oriented ventilator shaft confirmed the hunch. She swept the beam. A raised adobe bench, about eighteen inches high and a foot wide, encircled most of the kiva. The ventilator opening on the east was blocked by a damper stone, sealing it from exposure to the surface. What lay beyond the damper, Graciella did not venture to guess. West of the damper, the ladder holes, then a shallow adobe-lined ash pit. It still contained ashes, she realized!

A small slab air deflector, pecked to shape from a laminated tablet of garnet schist, was inserted into the union of the circles that defined the ash pit and hearth. The latter, lined with sandstone slabs, was curbed with a low, rounded layer of adobe. It was blackened from fire, but no charcoal or ash remained within its interior. It appeared to have been cleaned after it last burned. Grace's flash beam caught only one object within it. A small grey-and-white feather.

She reached it and held it up through the opening. "Ben," she asked, "is this what you were looking for?"

He took it from her. Graciella spent several more minutes taking flash pictures with Greg's camera. They lifted her out as thunder echoed over the eastern rise. It was now three-thirty. Graciella squinted from the light, then noted the dark clouds on the near horizon. "Let's cover it," she said.

Greg and Pete Montoya had already unfolded a large sheet of black plastic, and they all placed it as well as they could over the depression, weighting it with whatever they could find. The wind was kicking up occasional untethered rabbit brush and whooshing them softly across the landscape as tumbleweed.

"Okay, Ben," Pete said. "I'm headin' back." He hurried down the mound as the wind followed him in tiny swirls of dust. "Don't get wet, now," he yelled back. "I want the Captain to see you with that face!"

The three of them gathered the few tools Greg had brought and threw them in the back of the Bronco. Greg untied the block and tackle from the backhoe and added it to the pile. "Grace, we'll leave the backhoe here tonight," Greg said, pocketing the keys. "Just remind me to bring the grease-gun out tomorrow morning." The backhoe's working parts demanded lubrication after each use.

Graciella turned to Ben. "We'll be continuing this tomorrow morning," she smiled. "Care to join us again?"

Ben held up his hands mockingly. "I've had enough," he said. "Found exactly the items I expected to find, but thanks anyway."

Graciella smiled through a very dirty face. "The feather," she said, "and what else?"

"And no trowel," Ben answered, with an equally dirty smile.

Graciella gave him a humorously puzzled look. "You'll have to explain that to me, Ben Sandoval," she said.

"I will," Ben said, as the first drops began to fall. He turned to walk to his pickup. "When it's drier and we're both cleaner," he called back.

Graciella felt the cooling drops of moisture on her face. She stood watching Ben get into his pickup, wondering what he was really like underneath that professional veneer.

15

It was one-thirty and the lunch crowd was beginning to thin. Maria took a table at the end of the outdoor terrace in Ogilvie's, the second-floor restaurant that overlooked the Taos town plaza on the east side. She ordered a caesar's salad and a glass of white wine and looked out on the brick-paved plaza. Its trees provided shade for the small groups of locals and tourists who sat on its benches, and Maria was grateful that pedestrian and vehicle traffic was light and reasonably quiet. She felt emotionally exhausted.

She had driven to the Pueblo Clinic after breakfast to put in a few hours of volunteer work and to pay her respects to Anita's family and friends. The clinic staff was in a somber mood. She had dispatched an Indian girl to inquire if Anita's mother would receive her, but had been told that Anita's body was being returned to the Pueblo and her mother could see no one. The body would be dressed in Anita's finest white dress, with her shawl wrapped around her and wearing the traditional boots. Her hair would be carefully combed and set with ribbons, and cleansing rituals performed in preparation for burial, which would be today.

The doctor and nurse quizzed Maria about the murder and about the events leading up to it. What had drawn Anita to the excavation? Did the police have any suspects? Maria told them little, and nothing of her conversations with Anita. She and Anita had struck up a casual friendship over the past year, with Maria's interest in traditional medicine overlapping Anita's interest in the ancient traditions of her people. The friendship had remained rather distant, however. Anita was mostly closed in and secretive, volunteering little and responding to questions politely but with reserve. Her interest in Pot Creek had developed after she had visited the site during its annual summer open-house last year.

Maria took a sip of her wine and rotated the glass idly as she reflected. Apparently neither Greg nor Graciella had remembered her visit—dozens of visitors had been there. Greg had explained the work they were doing to the groups who came and went, and had indicated their intent to excavate the kiva below the rooms.

This was what had interested Anita. At the Clinic, she had asked Maria about the excavation and about the other kivas excavated. Maria had loaned Anita copies of the publications on Pot Creek, and had encouraged her to visit again and ask Greg the questions Maria could not answer.

Anita had never done so. In one conversation last winter she had asked whether the unexcavated kiva would be excavated this year, and had made vague reference to a "North Side Kiva" in legends of the Pueblo origin. When Maria had probed her, she had said a Picuris friend had told her, but Anita had been reluctant to discuss it. She had not mentioned Pot Creek again, except to tell Maria she had visited the open-house again this year. This had been in early July.

Maria pondered the recollection. Should she tell Lieutenant Sandoval about this? Probably so, she thought. She had seen him from a distance at the Pueblo this morning, accompanying the ambulance with Anita's body. He had left shortly afterwards. The Clinic doctor told her Sandoval had visited the day before, inquiring about both Anita and Maria.

There had been little to do at the Clinic, and Maria had checked patient records to compile the monthly Indian Health Service report. Then at ten, Anita's older brother had come in. She had met Luis Lujan before; he would come in occasionally to talk to his sister. This time he had wanted to see Maria.

Maria had expressed her sadness and asked if there were anything she could do. "Yes," he had said. "You can tell your husband that my brother and I must come to Pot Creek. To the place Anita died." His cold black eyes penetrated her knowing look. "We must make a ceremony there, alone," he had said. "Tell him we will come tomorrow."

Maria had been sympathetic. Of course they could come. But the police had the site taped off. Even her husband could not go there. Luis should contact Lieutenant Sandoval. Luis had said he would get the Lieutenant Governor to call. Then he had left. After that, the Clinic had closed in preparation for the burial.

Maria had attended the church ceremony in the San Geronimo mission, which had been mournful and emotional. Burial had been in the old churchyard, by the ruins of the original mission that was destroyed in the 1847 Taos Rebellion. Maria had not attended the burial. Rituals of mourning, purifying, and exorcising would continue for several days. She was relieved that today was Friday. It had been a week she would not wish to repeat.

The meeting with Graciella had been most disturbing of all. Maria had known for some time that Graciella was very suggestible and had a rich imagination. The ghost story she had told that evening a year ago had been quite realistic. Even in the highly charged atmosphere, the story had more than a ring of authenticity about it. Maria had become convinced then that Graciella had an almost clairvoyant quality about her. The test yesterday had confirmed even more: she had been unwilling to accept Maria's quite rational suggestion that the visions were imaginative. Indeed, Graciella's ability to effect a "cure" of her lesions, and her control of Maria's own memory, were startling confirmations of a rare ability.

Maria picked at her plate with the fork. Her past work with native curers involving trances and hallucinogenic plants had revealed certain suggestible personality types that were drawn towards shamanism. Aside from the obvious enhancement that came from sensory deprivation and drug-induced sensitivity, she knew that there were practitioners who required none of these accoutrements. Graciella was one of those, Maria thought. And she well understood that Graciella wielded a double-edged sword.

Maria finished her wine and got up. Most of the salad remained uneaten. She paid her bill and left.

◇◇◇

Andrea Abbott took her lunch break at one o'clock. The state archeologist's crew had wanted to finish a couple of one-meter-square test pits alongside the surveyed highway expansion before stopping. These were the last two for the week, since it was Friday, and no new excavations would be started until Monday. Red flagged pins in the distance along the right-of-way marked additional areas to be tested—areas whose surface features had indicated possible underlying archeological remains.

The crew had finished at 12:50 and had packed up their supplies and equipment. Andy had done the same, and decided to drive up to Picuris to have lunch in the snack bar at the pueblo. Although she had packed a sandwich and chips, she had yearned for a hamburger and cold drink.

She topped the rise and began descending into the small valley. Picuris Pueblo lay ahead, its one-story adobe houses clustered around and behind the church. In front of it was the broad dusty expanse where San Lorenzo Day festivals were held. A dirt road ran along and in front of this, at the end of which was the small museum, convenience store, and snack bar. Andy pulled up beside two other cars and went in.

The snack bar was behind the store. She had been here on numerous occasions during the month-long project, and her face was well-known. Andy was tall, slender, and very blonde, and would have stood out in almost any crowd. The clerk at the register smiled at her and took her order. Andy walked to a small table with her coke, took off her hat, and sat down. Her long blond hair had been pulled back into a ponytail, and she now took out the clasp and ran fingers through her hair, shaking it out. There were few people in the snack bar. Two teen-age Picuris Indians sat a few tables away and a tourist couple had been sitting at the table next to her and now they were walking through the small museum whose entry was off the snack bar. An old Indian man sat at a corner table, watching her occasionally. Her hamburger was brought to her, and she ate it slowly. One more week, she thought, and she would be returning to school. Greg would be out on Monday to review the work she had been doing. She would bring her final report to him back at SMU, where she would begin her last year of classes. She sipped her coke and glanced over to the corner. The old man was still looking at her. Had she seen him before?

Occasionally during the day, young Indian boys on their bicycles would visit the test pits where she and the others were working, and once or twice elders would stop and talk. The highway expansion was technically on Picuris land, but not on the pueblo itself, and some of the residents were idly curious. She did not remember him.

As she finished her hamburger, he rose and came over. "Excuse me," he said, "you are with the group at Fort Burgwin?"

"Yes, I am," she said. "I'm Andrea Abbott." She offered her hand.

He shook her hand and sat down. "I'm Joseph Espinosa," he said. His deeply lined face and deep set eyes betrayed no expression. He was probably in his seventies, Andy surmised. His hair was almost white, worn in two long braids that fell over his shoulders. "My son works at the Pot Creek Center sometimes," he said. "I heard about the murder of that Taos girl. Did you know her?"

"No," said Andy. "She used to work at the Indian Clinic, though, and our Director's wife, Maria Stern, knew her. It was terrible." Andy looked at him. "Did you know her?"

"I saw her a few times," Espinosa said. "Are they still excavating at Pot Creek?"

"I was told they were going to begin again this afternoon," Andy replied. "My professor, Greg Parson, and a student are working there."

Espinosa was quiet a moment. Then he looked up at Andy. "This student—Graciella is her name?—she was the one who was in the hospital. Is that so?"

Andy looked surprised. "Yes," she said, "how did you know? Do you know Graciella?"

"I never met her," Espinosa said. "Maybe you will see her when you go back today." He paused, as if indecisive. "Tell her she must be careful. Tell her there are dangers in what she is doing."

"Dangers?" Andy became uneasy. Is this a superstitious old man, she wondered? How do I respond here? "What kind of dangers?"

Espinosa gave her an angry look. "It is not my business," he said. "It is not yours, either. It is hers. Just tell her." He got up abruptly. "Just tell her," he repeated, nervously. He walked out without looking back.

◇◇◇

Graciella had showered and changed, and she and Greg had completed their field notes for the day. They sat in the archeology lab as the afternoon rain abruptly stopped and the sun reappeared. Greg was in an exhilarated mood as he and Graciella re-examined her theory in the aftermath of their brief work at the site.

"All right, Grace," he said. "Tomorrow we'll have Felix bring some four-by-fours. We'll widen the opening enough for me to get through it. Then we'll begin reinforcing the roof." He went to the door and looked out. "I don't think this little rain did any damage," he turned to her. "But we've got to be sure it's safe to work in the kiva. We don't want another collapse."

"Greg, I'm uncomfortable leaving the site unguarded tonight," she said. "Someone didn't want that excavation to get underway. I need to be out there."

"No, Grace," he said. "I'll admit that's a mystery, but no one has done anything since that first day." He returned to the table where they were working and sat down. "Look," he said. "I'll run over there on the way to dinner." He looked at his watch. Almost five. "I want to make sure the plastic held, anyway. I'll check it again after dinner, too," he said. "After that, it should be safe. We'll ask Karen and the students to be on the watch for any traffic on the road to the site."

Graciella looked a bit relieved. "Okay, Greg," she said. She glanced at him hesitantly. "After we're done tomorrow," she said, "I'd like to spend some time there, alone. Sort things out. Is that all right?"

He smiled and touched her hand. "It's fine, Grace," he said. "I know you've got this. . .personal. . ." he paused, almost said 'emotional' ". . .involvement over there. Maybe you'll explain it to me someday. I want it to be over for you."

She smiled back. "Thanks, Greg. I don't know what it is. I've had some strange experiences. . .probably only my imagination. . .since that first excavation. Maybe some time alone there will help me straighten it all out."

Greg sat back. "Well, I've got to go with Danny to Miranda Canyon tomorrow afternoon, anyway," he said. "Then Monday I'll be with Andy for awhile. I hope we can get our work done at the kiva by noon tomorrow. Come Tuesday, I need to fly back to Dallas." He got up. "Time for dinner. You print this report while I drive over to the site, okay?"

As he left, Andy Abbott walked in with her field pack. "Hi, Grace," she nodded, putting the pack on the long table. "Glad I caught you. I have a sinister message for you from Picuris." She sat on the table and related the incident in the Picuris snack bar. When she finished, she spread her hands in bewilderment, ". . .and then he just got up and left. Not even a 'goodbye' or anything! What do you make of that?"

"I have no clue, Andy," Graciella said. "How did he know my name, I wonder?" If his son works at the Cultural Site, she thought, I may have seen him there. "Did he mention his son's name?" Graciella asked.

"No," Andy said. "But I'll tell you, he was serious! Almost gave me the creeps." She looked at Graciella. "Aren't you afraid, Grace? Maybe you'd better tell that detective."

Graciella thought about it a moment. "Maybe I will," she said. "I'll be all right, Andy," she smiled. "Probably just an old man who believes in evil spirits. Anita's death—to many in the pueblos, a witch or spirit caused it, I guess."

"Maybe so," Andy said. She finished unpacking her supplies and putting them in the cabinet above the counter. "But you be careful, anyway," she said, turning to leave.

"Oh, Andy," Graciella said. "Keep an ear open tonight. If you hear or see anyone on the road to Pot Creek, come tell Greg or me, okay? And tell Danny to be on guard, too."

"Right," Andy said, and left.

A chill came over her as she sat alone in the lab. She was now frightened. Whether the old man was sending a threat or a warning, this was now a dangerous situation, she thought. She needed protection—whether from ghosts of the past or from some crazed killer in human form.

◇◇◇

Ghost stories. Her mind went back to the campfire early this summer. It had been her second experience with the visions, and as Maria had said, the group clustered before the fire had listened as if it were a well-told story from Graciella's imagination. Only Maria had detected something more. How had she?

There had been six or eight of them, students mostly. Ned had brought his guitar. The fire in the corner fireplace of the fort patio had burned brightly as the group had sung folk songs. As the twilight receded and stars appeared in the darkening sky, the group began exchanging ghost stories. The fire slowly died down, casting a faint glow on their faces, and as the farther reaches of the patio became absorbed in blackness Graciella began her story and the vision took its shape. The scent of juniper and sage was faintly present as she spoke.

The kiva fire burns softly as the priest kneels on its west, and continues now the pattern with the pollen gently held;

and the line now passes on its floor, from Shipap to the hearth; a narrow highway to this world from worlds below and dark.

The sipapu would open soon,
but only if the song was right,
and only if the altar stone
held what the legends told.

And if it did, and if the song was faithful and exact,
and if the line of sacred grain was laid to north and south, then life would
join with death once more. Then day would follow night.
The priest moves quietly across and sits beside the hearth, and on the south
red corn is laid, from kiva wall to fire.
Its kernels faintly visible, its line precisely straight, symbolic of the blood of
life as warmth replaces cold
and living tissue grows within. Now moving to the north, white kernels laid
with equal care define the second part:
the breath of life, in purity and coolness, joined with blood,
will warm and quicken and create—once more—our people. . . .
Silence. Each face focuses upon the altar stone,
the faces of the elders circled round the kiva wall.
The smoke now rising through the roof,
through the sky and up beyond,
will carry soon our ancient kin:
our spirits joined.
To celebrate our journey here,
to bring our lives together here,
to give this place its sacred name:
to bring us home.
The song begins, so softly now and scarcely heard, but rising.
With water from the sacred spring, the priest moves quickly, pouring. . .
carefully. . .the line that runs from hearth to eastern wall: The final part is
done.
Now warmth of blood and breath of life
can join with water and call back
our women from beyond the past,
from Shipap's womb.
The priest now kneels behind the fire, facing west, and reaches over,
placing sacred objects now upon the altar, and begins.
The sacred chant so long remembered, long unspoken, on this night
will send its power down and under, calling forth our ancient daughters. . .
come and seek us. . .
Emerging from the sipapu a narrow shaft of light
swiftly follows sacred pollen,
brightens as it strikes the altar!
Bifurcating north and south,

they strike each kernel as they travel.
Converging, now, upon the hearth the shafts explode in fire and thunder!
Brightness briefly blinds the elders, and the shafts of light, now single,
climb the smoky column upward. . .through the timbers. . .and are gone.
Stunned to silence, in their places, all the elders fix their vision
on the darkened scene before them—fearing yet to voice their horror:

blackened streak where pollen smoulders;
kernels charred from north to south;
rising steam from sacred water,
Now released.

In the center—on the ash pit—
softly lit by muted embers
lies the lifeless, naked body
of the priest.

Contours dancing from reflection
of the dying hearth beside it,
it bears features of a stranger,
not a brother!

The elders rise and stand around it.
Not a priest, this broken body,
nor an elder of this kiva
nor another!

Young and lithe, this twisted body,
not a clansman of their people.
Softly built, this headless torso —
now an omen.

We have lost, an elder whispers,
peering down at fragile features,
youthful breasts and supple contours
of a woman!

Graciella had been caught up in the story-telling spirit on the occasion when this had come to her, and had not been frightened by it or by the knowledge that this had been told through her as much as by her. Now, she realized, she was indeed afraid. She would go to the faculty office and call Ben.

As she locked the lab to leave, she had the chilling thought that the young woman in her vision could be—might have been—herself.

16

As Graciella left the lab and walked towards the fort, Maria called to her from across the parade ground. "Graciella, I need to talk to you," she said, approaching. "Lieutenant Sandoval phoned," she said, holding a message slip out to her. "He wants you to call him."

"I was just going up to the office to call him," Graciella said. "Something frightening is going on, Maria." Her voice was uneasy as she spoke.

"Graciella, you're white as a sheet," Maria said. "Come, use the phone in our quarters." She guided Graciella by the arm. "I need to tell you some things, and the Lieutenant, as well."

They went inside, where Horace stood waiting. "Ladies," he said, "shall we go to dinner? It's after five."

"You go ahead and we'll join you later," Maria said. "Graciella needs to return the Lieutenant's call." Horace left and Graciella dialed the number on the message slip.

"Sandoval," the voice answered.

"Lieutenant. . .Ben. . .it's Graciella."

"Yes, Graciella," his voice softened. "I wanted to tell you that Luis Lujan and his brother want to come out to Pot Creek tomorrow. They need to spend some time alone at the excavation. It's important to them. Will this be okay?"

"Ben," Graciella said. "Yes. But I need to talk to you. I'm frightened. I was sent a warning today from Picuris."

"What kind of warning?" Ben asked. "Who sent it?"

"It's involved, Ben," Graciella said. "Someone whose son works at the Cultural Center. Said what I was doing was dangerous, and to be careful." She hesitated. "Ben, I have some other things to tell you. Can I see you?"

"I'll be right out," Ben said without hesitation. "Where will you be?"

She looked at Maria, who was gesturing that she wanted to speak to him. "I'm in the Commander's Quarters," she said. "With Maria Stern. She wants to talk to you as well."

"Fifteen minutes," Ben said. He hung up.

Maria guided Graciella to the sofa. "Sit down," she said. "Tell me about this warning! What can I get you?"

"I could really use a drink, Maria," she said. "Anything strong!"

Maria brought them each a gin and tonic and sat down. Graciella recounted what Andy had told her. "Maria," she said finally, "I'm going to tell Ben about my visions. Everything that has happened to me. Did you know Anita was at Pot Creek when I had the accident? I think it was her scream that you heard."

Maria looked startled. "What? It wasn't your scream?"

Graciella told her of her conversation with Ben Sandoval. "I'm at the center of all this, Maria," she concluded. "Everything points to me. Even you hinted at that earlier. You must tell me what you know about this!"

Maria sat forward. "Yes, Graciella," she said, reaching for her hand. "After this morning at the Pueblo, I decided I'd better tell you and the Lieutenant more about Anita Lujan." She related her past conversations with Anita, Anita's interest in Pot Creek, her visits to the site and her reluctance, when Maria had suggested it, to visit with either Greg or Graciella. "It was some mystical thing with her, Graciella," Maria said. "She was very closed in about it, very private. But she sometimes seemed intense."

"Why did you think someone was trying to prevent me from excavating?" Graciella asked.

"I just had this feeling," Maria said. "I was pretty certain no one here had filled in your site Monday night. Anita was the only connection." She gave Graciella a frustrated look. "I thought maybe Anita had done it. But I didn't know why." Maria sat back and said, tentatively, "After our conversation yesterday, I'm convinced that something mystical is happening to you, Graciella. I'm now wondering whether Anita may have, somehow, known about all this."

"That could have terrifying consequences for me," Graciella said, and shuddered. "As it did for her. I'm really frightened."

Maria got up to refresh their drinks, and as she came back there was a knock on the door. Graciella took a sip as Maria returned, followed by Ben. He smiled, "Well, you both look pretty grim."

Graciella was noticeably relieved at Ben's arrival and gave him a half-hearted smile. "Ben, I don't want to sound hysterical, but I really think I'm in danger." She told him about Andy's conversation with the old man. "What's so frightening is how he got my name," she said.

"Joseph Espinosa," Ben said. "Joe Espinosa must be his son. He's been volunteering at the Cultural Site; was there the morning of the murder. Have you met him?"

"No," said Graciella, "I don't think so."

"Graciella, I think you and I are going to Picuris tomorrow," he said.

"Ben, I can't," Graciella pleaded. "Greg and I have to stabilize the kiva tomorrow. Can't you go alone?"

"<u>You</u> have to talk to Espinosa, Graciella," Ben said. "I doubt he'd talk to me. Even if I weren't the law." He became solemn. "This could be very important, Graciella. To both of us. Miss Abbott told you he had seen Anita—chances are he knew her."

Maria broke in. "She had been to Picuris, Lieutenant. She told me once about a legend she heard from a Picuris friend." Maria related all that she had told Graciella about Anita Lujan, ending with her brief conversation with Luis Lujan this morning.

"All right," Ben said when she had finished. "Maybe I can begin to put things together now." He looked at her sternly. "But I wish you had told me about Anita earlier. You must understand: the more I know about Anita's motives, the more I'll know about her murderer's. They're very reluctant to talk at the Pueblo."

Graciella looked at him intently. He was right, she thought to herself. And the more he knows, the safer I'll be. "Ben, I think you'd better come with me." She got up and glanced furtively at Maria, who nodded. "I have something you need to hear."

Maria saw them out, and Graciella and Ben walked to her apartment. Inside, she went to her bookshelf and took down three audio-cassette tapes. She sat, holding the tapes and going through her thoughts, trying to decide the best way to say this.

"Ben," she said, "I'm a reasonably intelligent person. I think I'm also reasonably sane. I'm not superstitious, not even religious. I never indulge in fantasies." She looked at him, saw that he was listening intently. "But," she said, "something happened at the site last year, an experience, that began a chain of events which I believe led to Anita's murder." She told him briefly about the initial sensation in Room 703, about the journeys into the other reality, about her compulsion to re-excavate and find the kiva, and finally about the underground pressure released with her pick as the room collapsed upon her.

Throughout, Ben remained impassive but attentive. When she finished, she held up the tapes. "Ben, each of these journeys is recorded here. I have remembered each minute detail, even languages I don't speak. I have recorded each one after it happened." She handed the tapes to him. "Don't say anything. Don't tell me I'm crazy or sane. Take them home. Listen to them."

Ben got up and went to the door. "Eight-thirty tomorrow," he said. "I'll be here." He waved the tapes. "Thanks. Lock your door."

She nodded, and he was gone. After a while she locked the door, got undressed and crawled into bed. She left the desk light on.

16

It was just after eight on Saturday morning and Greg sat with Danny Sheffield at breakfast. "Sorry to get you up for this," Greg said. "I intended to get Felix to help me at the site, but he's going to Santa Fe."

Lieutenant Sandoval had sought Greg out at the Dining Hall last night after leaving Graciella. He had explained their trip to Picuris this morning and, under the circumstances, Greg could hardly object. Besides, shoring up the kiva roof would require some heavy lifting, for which Danny was better suited. Felix had seemed delighted that Graciella was not going to work the site today, and had promised to deliver the lumber before he left the fort.

"I'll be glad to help, Greg," Danny said. "When we finish we can go directly to Miranda Canyon, if you like." Danny brushed a sweep of his straight brown hair out of his face and continued eating. He was tall and thin, and his face had a sallow, almost gaunt, look. Not particularly strong, perhaps, Greg thought, but certainly tall enough to help wedge supports under the sagging roof.

Graciella came through the cafeteria line, spotted them, and hurried over. "Oh, Greg, I'm glad I caught you," she said. "I've got a problem with this morning. Lieutenant Sandoval. . ."

". . .has already talked to me about it," Greg finished. "It's fine. Sit down. Danny will give me a hand."

"Thanks, Danny," she said, sitting. "I owe you. Greg," she turned to him, "you won't do any excavating, will you?"

"Just clean-up, Grace," he said. "We'll widen the entrance, make certain the roof is completely stable, and clear out all the fallen debris." He smiled, "The site is fine, by the way. I checked it before coming to breakfast."

Danny looked at Graciella sympathetically. "Andy told us about that weird warning, Grace," he said. "Last night at dinner. Is that why you're going to Picuris?"

"Well," said Graciella, "I'm going mainly because Lieutenant Sandoval insisted. I'd _much_ rather be at the site."

Greg looked up. "By the way, Grace," he said. "Sandoval says the Lujan brothers will be out sometime later today. I told him someone would show them to the site, then leave them."

"Yes," Graciella said. "If I'm here, I'll be happy to." She got up and went in for a second helping of eggs and bacon. She was famished. She had not eaten dinner last night, and couldn't recall eating lunch, either. Too upset for food last night, the dreamless sleep and prospects for resolving this today combined to freshen her perspective and her appetite. Or was it, she wondered, the prospect of having a fascinating detective as a sympathetic ally, able to protect her from spirits and witches?

She returned to the table just as Ben entered the foyer. He spotted her and came over, pausing to pour a styrofoam cup of coffee. He wore jeans and boots with a black western shirt and black Navajo-style hat: broad, flat brim with high, unblocked crown. The hat band sported a single row of buffalo-nickel conchas. He looked truly Indian. And no badge.

He nodded good morning to them all as he sat opposite Graciella. "I came early," he said, raising his cup. "Tired of instant coffee." He took a tentative sip, sat back, and smiled. "Everything all right overnight?" he asked.

"The site is intact, Lieutenant," Greg said. "I was there a few minutes ago."

"And we're going over now to begin our work," Danny added, rising with his tray. "Grace, good luck," he said.

Greg rose also. "Lieutenant, Grace," he nodded. "I hope all this is over soon." To Graciella, he said "See you this evening, if not earlier." The two of them left.

Ben smiled across at her. "I count only one person here who calls you 'Graciella'," he said. "Maria Stern."

She thought a moment. "Actually," she said, "there are three. I haven't pushed it, though. After all, I first registered at school as Grace. I know who I am," she smiled, "at least most of the time."

"And you slept okay? No problems?"

"None," she said. "I'm still frightened. But I'm rested." She had finished her eggs, was now munching the last of the bacon. He sat silently, sipping his coffee. She took her tray up and returned with a coffee refill. She looked at Ben, trying to read his mood, and his reaction to the tapes she loaned him. "Well," she said finally, "say something to me."

Ben shifted his chair back. "Let's ride," he said. "We'll talk."

The loose gravel kicked up a little as the pickup weaved its way from the Dining Hall, among the junipers, out to the highway. They turned right, heading towards U.S. Hill and Peñasco. The sun, to their left, was now above the rise of the highest peaks, its brightness muted by remnant wisps of morning clouds that would shortly burn off.

"Graciella," Ben asked, "are you familiar with the 'vision quest'?"

Graciella looked over at him curiously, but he kept his eyes on the road ahead. "A little," she said. "I believe the Plains Indians practiced it. A young boy would go out alone, without food, until a spirit came to him in a vision."

"Something like that," Ben said. "Different tribes had variations on it. Basically it was the proper way to seek one's guardian spirit." He looked over at her. "My people—the Jicarilla—didn't practice this. But I heard about it as a child. It was appealing. To have your own identity through a personal animal, or plant, or star. A lucky star." He focused back on the highway as they began the twisted climb to U.S. Hill. "So when I was about twelve, I decided to go on a vision quest. I packed a bedroll, took my horse, and went up to La Jara Lake. About fifteen miles from our horse ranch. Stayed there two nights. Fished for my meals, walked into the forest, sat in my camp overlooking the lake, communed with nature." He paused, negotiating the next to last curve before reaching the top. An RV was ahead of them, laboring steadily, and Ben slowed.

"And did you have your vision?" Graciella asked, finally.

"I did not," Ben said. "Middle of the third day, I started back down. I was angry with myself, and embarrassed that I had not succeeded. Then I figured I was being childish. Apaches don't go on vision quests, I thought. We don't need guardian spirits to protect us. Why should I be any different? I rode in to the ranch. I was hungry, hadn't caught many fish, and my mother made a meal for me. We sat at the table, my mother and father and me, and they didn't ask me anything. They carried on like I'd been there the whole time." Ben smiled to himself at the recollection. "Then my father put some leftovers in a bowl and asked me to give him a hand. We went out back to small chicken-wire pen my father had built that morning. He had come upon a young golden eagle with a broken wing. That eagle was in the pen, a splint on its wing, all bandaged, wanting to fly away but not able to. My father told me, 'You'll have to take care of him for awhile.' He was taking some horses into Farmington for the next couple of days."

They passed the R.V. on a straight stretch of highway and began climbing toward the final curve. Ben looked over at Graciella. "When the wing healed and I let him loose, that eagle would come back every now and then." He smiled. "I figured he'd come looking for me while I was out looking for him."

They reached the crest in silence, and Graciella turned to him. "Everyone wants to speak to me in riddles," she said in frustration. "First Maria, now you. Ben Sandoval, did you listen to my tapes? Do you believe I actually saw and heard these things? Or do you think I'm just giving a mystical interpretation to something as mundane as an eagle with a broken wing?"

Ben pulled into the parking area at the vista point and came to a stop. "Get out," he said. They walked to the stone embankment beyond the Forest Service sign. Beyond them lay the high valley where the Rio Grande del Rancho— the "Little Rio"—begins its course down to the Taos Plateau. Looking into the valley where they began their climb, they could see the distant clearing across from the fort and the nested hills where Pot Creek leaves its mountain haven to join the Little Rio. On the horizon they could see the hazy outlines of New Mexico's highest mountains, where Blue Lake lay hidden.

Ben gestured towards the scene beyond them. "Graciella," he said, "look out there. We're surrounded by a familiar landscape, right? It's known, it's been studied, and we understand it, wouldn't you say?"

"Of course, Ben," she said.

"Wrong," Ben looked at her. "Parts of it are familiar. Parts have been studied. Most have not." He looked out again. "There may be a dozen golden eagles out there, probably less. Most of us never see one, or don't know it if we do. There are species out there, plants and animals, which have *never* been seen by anyone. Truth is," he turned to her, "we're surrounded by the *unfamil-iar*. We only recognize the familiar, because it's what we look for; because it's what we expect."

Graciella gave him a wry smile. "Okay, so you're an Apache philosopher, as well," she said. "What I have experienced is not just an unfamiliar part of *that* reality," she gestured towards the distant hills.

"What do you want from me?" Ben asked. "What reaction are you looking for?"

"I want you to say 'Yes, Graciella; you've really taken those journeys—not in your mind, but in real space and time.' *That's* what I want to hear!"

He laughed. "You're a true scientist, aren't you?" he said. "For you, reality is what others can confirm. You explain your kiva's existence with a hypothesis that can be tested by science. You demand a reality that conforms."

"My reality, Ben, does *not* conform!" Graciella's voice strained. "What I demand is an understanding of that reality, in terms I can handle!"

"From what I heard on those tapes, Graciella, you had very clear understanding," Ben said. "You were not confused, not troubled by the events which occurred. . . ."

"Not *when* they occurred, Ben, but afterwards," Graciella stared at him. "Those journeys were not isolated. They all have links to here and now."

Ben took her by the shoulders. "Yes, they do," he said to her. "So there are not two realities, Graciella. There is only one. Maybe those links are all the confirmation you need." He smiled and turned again to the distant mountains. "But me, I can only confirm the here and now." He sensed in her eyes a sense of disappointment that he had not given her what she needed. "My job is to search for links, Graciella," he said. "Anita's death was real, and if it is linked to the other side of this reality, we'll find it." He looked directly into her eyes. "Reality expands as the unfamiliar becomes familiar. Making it familiar is one way to eliminate fear."

She leaned against him, her head on his chest, trembling slightly as she tried to resist the tears. "Then help me, Ben," her voice broke. "Help me on this side of that reality."

He held her, stroking her hair, until the tears were gone and the trembling stopped.

◇◇◇

When they arrived at Picuris and parked at the Governor's office the sky was cloudless and the sun bright. They had agreed that Ben would accompany her only to the office, and that she would seek out Joseph Espinosa alone. Ben went over the specific information she was to try to get from him, coaching her on how to ask questions indirectly, encouraging her to be patient and deliberate, assuring her that she would be in no danger from the old man. He would make his own inquiries of the Governor, or of any other officials who were available.

Graciella got directions to Espinosa's house. It was back beyond the church to the left, in the older part of the pueblo. A few residents were outside their houses and glanced at her curiously as she walked by, and she tried to appear casual, as if the place were familiar. She found the old adobe without difficulty. Across an open plaza from it was the old Scalp House, its single main viga projecting out the rear for some ten feet, supported there by the single center-post of the adjacent room whose walls had long since crumbled.

She knocked on the door, and the elderly woman who answered it showed no curiosity as she looked at Graciella. "I'm very sorry to disturb you," Graciella said. "I'm looking for Joseph Espinosa."

"My son, Joe?" the old woman asked.

"No, ma'am," Graciella said. "Your. . .the elder Joseph."

The old woman disappeared inside, and shortly an old man came to the door. "I'm Joseph Espinosa," he said. His small, deep eyes fixed on her face.

"Mr. Espinosa," she said, "My name is Graciella. I'm from Pot Creek. My friend, Andrea Abbott, spoke with you yesterday."

"She did," he nodded. There was no surprise in his voice.

"I am grateful that you were concerned enough to talk to her," Graciella said softly. "I thought perhaps you would talk to me as well."

The old man hesitated. He turned and went back into the room. Graciella could not see far into the darkened interior, but could hear him saying something in Tiwa to the old woman. Presently he returned, opened the door, and stepped outside.

"Yes," he sighed, not looking at her, and began to walk slowly across the small plaza. He turned and indicated for Graciella to follow him. They stopped at the ruined wall behind the ancient Scalp House. "Years ago, some of your people came here," he said. "From Fort Burgwin. They helped us excavate some of the old ruins," he indicated the area behind them. "They helped us build our museum, and told us about our own origins at Pot Creek." He turned his weathered face toward her, his long white braids falling over his shoulders. "Of course, we already knew this. But it was important to have scientists show what our history told us. We appreciate what you have been doing."

He sat on the wall, and Graciella did the same. He looked back across the plaza at the row of adobe houses. "Some people, they say we are a dying pueblo," he said. "Not so big, like Taos. Not so pretty. The young people, even at Taos, they want better houses, they want better jobs. So they leave the pueblo. We raise buffalo now, and we own a big hotel down in Santa Fe, and encourage our young people to stay and help build back our community." He looked at her. "Some of our young people, at Taos, too, they have taken an interest in our past—like you have—and teach the children some of our old ways." He paused, looked away. "Like Anita Lujan, and my son Joe."

"Did you know Anita?" Graciella asked.

"I knew her," he answered. "She came here sometimes, even at our ceremonies. She talked to some of us old ones, wanting to learn stories and songs. She said our two peoples, Taos and Picuris, were once together and we should share our common traditions." He paused. "Some people do not want this. They believe we were always two peoples; that we were enemies. Others believe that we became enemies when we left Pot Creek. This is what Anita believed." He paused again. "It is what killed her."

Graciella looked at him abruptly. His eyes were fixed on the ground, now, and he said nothing. Graciella waited. Finally, she said, "How did that belief kill her, Mr. Espinosa?"

He coughed and slowly stood. "In our ancient legends, there is one about how we became divided, Taos and Picuris. We came together in the beginning as many people, many clans, joining from different places, as the village grew. The last of the clans came up from the South, from the waters beyond the Rio Grande. They were the strongest. They built their houses on the north end of the village and had their own kiva there, close to their houses. Their kiva society became the one that governed the village. Their ceremonies became the most important ones. Their kiva chief became the priest of the land, and the corn, and the sky. He had powers to enrich the land, and powers to change people into animals and water into fire."

The old man stopped abruptly and looked at Graciella. "I'm telling you too much," he said. "I cannot say any more. Anita thought you had found this kiva. She knew of the ceremony that destroyed the village and separated its people. Performed correctly, the ceremony might reunite the people." He turned away, facing the old ruins. "Someone, a *cahane*—a witch—one who can change into other things, did not want this ceremony to be performed. The witch killed her." He turned back to face Graciella. "The witch tried to stop you from digging that kiva. I think you should not dig any more there."

Graciella stood and looked at him, waited until his eyes met hers. "Do you know who this witch is?" she asked.

"Even if I did," the old man replied, "I could not say its name. It is dangerous to even talk about it."

He turned toward the Scalp House. "We have been enemies, Taos and Picuris, in the past," he said, "but not any longer. We do not need to face the anger of ancient spirits in the hope of reuniting us."

"Are there still those who consider you an enemy?" Graciella asked. "Do some at Picuris consider Taos the enemy?"

"There are," he replied. "At Taos there were once many scalps—Ute, Jicarilla—and some were Picuris. Here," he indicated the Scalp House, "we also had many. Most were Ute and Kiowa, some Commanche." He pulled out a bandana and wiped his face, then gave her a final look. "The first scalp was the head of a Taos woman. You must leave, now." The old man turned and walked slowly toward his adobe. Graciella stood silently, watching him until he disappeared inside.

17

On the ride back Graciella repeated what Espinosa had told her. Apparently, the kiva in the legend was the North Side Kiva that Anita had referred to cryptically when she had spoken with Maria. If Anita had believed this to be the under-room kiva they had exposed at Pot Creek, her interest in the site was understandable.

And also understandable, Ben remarked, was Anita's reluctance to talk to Graciella or Greg. A legend and a ceremony and a desire to repair what had happened in prehistory would not have fallen on sympathetic ears. It was not a matter for archeologists at all. It was of ritual, not scientific, importance.

Then she *had* been at the site that morning, waiting for Graciella to complete the subfloor exposure of the kiva. So she could perform the ceremony? Graciella wondered. A witch had killed her, Espinosa had said; the same witch who had filled in the excavation to prevent that exposure.

"He said I shouldn't dig any more there, Ben," Graciella said. "What about Greg and Danny? They're over there now. Are they in any danger?"

"We'll go directly there," Ben said. "But I think maybe Maria was right: it's *you* alone who this person wants to stop. Just as he stopped Anita. She had the ritual power this person was afraid of. Whoever killed her somehow knows that you, too, have some special power."

They were again at the vista on U.S. Hill, and now began the descent towards Pot Creek. "Graciella, tell me exactly who knows about your experiences with these visions," Ben said. "You've told Maria, but anyone else?"

"No one, Ben," Graciella said. "Greg knows about the first experience at the site, last year. He knows I've been obsessed with digging the kiva, but he thinks I'm imagining things."

"What about Felix and the workers, Graciella? Have you ever spoken with Alberto Sanistevan?"

"Who?" Graciella looked at him. "Alberto? I may have said a few words to him in the past. I don't remember. They're always around, working in the yard or on the buildings. Why?"

"I saw Alberto at Picuris," Ben said. "While you were meeting with Espinosa. He and Joe Espinosa, the son, left together. I asked about them in the office. Turns out Alberto is Joe's brother-in-law. I'm going to have another talk with him."

◇◇◇

It was eleven-thirty when they arrived at Pot Creek. Greg and Danny were just finishing their work. The entrance to the kiva, at the point of the original collapse, had been widened and the fallen viga was now back in position. A four-by-four support had been placed near the original post in the kiva floor and the viga rested on it. An additional support had been placed adjacent to the southwestern post to reinforce it. A four-foot square opening spanned the distance from the viga to the center of the curving kiva wall on the west, bordered by two additional timbers running from the viga to the wall. At the wall itself, these timbers rested on a four-by-four lying atop the wall at the surface. A ladder rested against it.

Greg and Danny were in the kiva, sweeping up the remaining debris. This would be loaded into buckets and removed. Except for the ventilator, the kiva was essentially excavated. It could now be studied in detail.

"It looks great, Greg," Graciella said.

Greg came up the ladder with a bucket. "Amazingly, most of the original timbers are in good shape, Grace," he said. "We've tested all the supports and vigas. They appear to be structurally sound. This is unbelievable!" He wiped his brow and reached for his canteen. "But I want to run flagging tape around the overlying rooms, just to keep anyone from walking there."

"I'll do that," Graciella said. "You and Danny go on to Miranda Canyon. Danny," she turned to him, "thanks again for helping."

Danny emptied his bucket on the backdirt pile. "Glad to help, Grace," he said. They all walked back towards the parked vehicles. "You can drive us both back in the Bronco and keep it. Greg and I will take mine."

"Greg," Graciella said, "when you get back, we need to talk."

"We all need to, Greg," Ben said. "The Lujan brothers will be here this evening, and I'll want to see all of you after I've spoken with them." He turned to Graciella. "Can you arrange a meeting, Graciella? Include Ned, Horace and Maria, the students, everyone. After dinner."

"Felix and the workers, too?" she asked.

"No," Ben said. "I'm going to Alberto's place in Ranchos now. Then I'll see Felix." He paused at his truck. "Get some lunch, Graciella," he said. "Don't come back to the site without me."

Graciella drove back with Greg and Danny, explaining briefly what Espinosa had told her. They both got her assurance that she would not go to the site alone. "Grace," Greg said as they parked next to the fort compound, "we need to put a barrier on the road over there. I don't want any unauthorized people at the site. It has absolutely unbelievable preservation!"

"I'll talk to Horace," Graciella said. "He can have Felix do it." As she got out she noticed the block-and-tackle had been left in the back of the Bronco. "I'll put this back, Greg," she said. "Where did you get it?"

"Felix got it for me," Greg said. "I believe it belongs in the tool room at the far corner." He and Danny left, and Graciella pulled the rope and pulleys out of the Bronco.

As she approached the office inside the compound, Horace and Karen were locking up for lunch. "Dr. Stern, I need to put this back," she said. "Could you unlock the tool room for me?"

"Certainly," he said. He walked with her. "Maria is fixing lunch for Karen and me. Why don't you join us?"

"Thanks," Graciella said. "I'll go down and clean up first. I need to talk to you."

He unlocked the padlock for her, then left with Karen. Graciella put her burden down inside the door and turned on the light. She looked around for a place. The rope and pulleys were probably not used much. Where should she put them? Along the far back wall to her left were broad shelves. One shelf was partially empty, with a coil of rope at one end. She edged her way back with the block-and-tackle and carefully coiled it and put it on the shelf. As she did so, a loose pulley fell to the floor. She knelt to retrieve it and noticed a dirty rag in the corner, partially covering two large mason's trowels and the handle of a smaller one. Curious, Graciella lifted the rag. She stared, then moved forward for a closer look. There was no mistaking the narrow blade, thinned from seasons of filing it down, its sharpened edges showing their metallic sheen even in the dim light of the room. Graciella involuntarily caught her breath as she jumped back. "Oh, my God!" she said in a whispered scream.

She quickly scrambled over the shovels and picks, turned out the light, and slammed the door shut. She padlocked it and leaned against it, as if holding back some unknown force within the room. She felt the weakness in her knees, the chill that coursed through her body even in the heat of mid-day. She hastily looked around. The compound was empty.

She closed her eyes tightly, her hand to her mouth, willing her stomach to forbear its threatened upheaval. Then she ran to the bathroom on the opposite side of the patio, closed and locked its door, and ran water in the basin, splashing it on her face. She toweled her face and looked at herself in the mirror. The bandage was coming loose again, and she tore it off. She appeared slightly pale. She sat down, face in hands, until her weakness began to subside. She removed her other bandages, looked at her reflection once more, then slowly unlocked and opened the door.

She stood listening. A magpie called from high in the cottonwood outside. Hummingbirds whistled back and forth, visiting the feeder by the office. No other sound. No other movement.. Graciella walked quickly outside the compound, and then towards the Commander's Quarters. To the safety of friends.

18

Ben drove down the dusty road that leads west from the Santa Fe highway and the Ranchos Post Office and out towards the vast Taos Plateau. Land holdings here ranged from large acreage, where alfalfa and cattle were raised, to small half-acre plots. Houses also ranged in style, from *moradas* to haciendas in the tradition of adobe architecture, and from house trailers to an imaginative assortment of shapes in concrete block, metal, and glass. A few earth-houses were buried into hillsides, only a single wall exposing their occupants to the world outside. Occasionally a polyhedron rose up from the landscape, each room with a unique view of mountains or plains.

Ben followed the directions given him at the post office, and after a few turns found it. Alberto Sanistevan lived in a house trailer that had been expanded by a concrete block addition that included a fireplace with chimney. Along the front of the house, and in two tractor tires converted into planters at each end, were petunias, larkspur, and other flowers in full bloom. Two Russian olive trees grew in the front yard. Beside the house was an old Ford pickup with its hood up. Alberto was bent over it working on the engine. He looked up as Ben pulled in.

"*Buenos dias*, Alberto," Ben said as he approached.

"Señor Lieutenant," Alberto said. "*¡Hola! ¿Qué passo?*"

"I saw you at Picuris earlier today," Ben said, casually. "With your brother-in-law."

"With Joe? *Sí*. We were getting some parts for my pickup." Alberto put down the distributor he had been working on and wiped his hands with a rag. "He has an old Ford over there. We use it for parts. What were you doing there?"

"Just visiting," Ben said. "I need to check with you about some things."

Alberto put the rag down and leaned with his arms on the fender. He looked at Ben with piercing black eyes that seemed to float on his round face. He was short, built solidly, and had the broad hands and thick upper arms of someone used to heavy labor. "*Sí*, Lieutenant?" he asked. "What things?"

"On the day of the accident at Pot Creek," Ben said. "You and Luis Garza and Felix were working together on the foot-bridge." Ben leaned on the opposite fender, facing Alberto. "Were you there all day, the three of you?"

"*Sí*, like we told you," Alberto said. "It was a big job. We didn't finish it until yesterday."

"What time did you start on Wednesday?"

"Let me think," Alberto hesitated. "That morning. . . ." He rubbed his moustache nervously. "*Sí*, I remember. I got there about 8:30 or 9:00, I guess. Joe brought me a load of firewood, I guess about 8:00. I was getting gas for my truck, and he was here when I got back. We unloaded the firewood." He looked at Ben. "Maybe it was just after nine when I got to the fort. Felix gave me the time off."

"Did you and Joe leave at the same time?"

"I probably left right after he did," Alberto said.

"Alberto, did you notice any vehicles parked at the Cultural Site when you passed? Joe's, or maybe a red Honda?"

"Yes, sir," Alberto replied. "Joe's truck was parked outside the gate. Didn't see no Honda, though."

Ben paused, picked up the distributor. "You good with this sort of thing?"

"*Sí*. Gotta be," Alberto said, relaxing a bit. "What Joe and me can't do, don't get done." He took the distributor. "But this, it's not hard to do, long as you know the wiring."

"Felix ever help you out?" Ben asked.

"Sometimes," Alberto said. "Mostly he works alone."

"Last Wednesday," Ben said. "Did any of you work alone? Even for a short time?"

"Well," Alberto said, "we had to work together putting that bridge together. At lunch Felix went home." He thought a moment. "Maybe a couple times one of us went to get something."

"Like what?" Ben said. "Try to remember, amigo."

Alberto looked nervous again. "Is it important?" he asked, scratching his moustache.

"Probably not," Ben smiled. He recalled the second rule of criminal investigations: Whatever detail seems unimportant, probably is.

"I guess I went to the tool shed a couple times," Alberto said. "Had to get a long extension cord for the drill, I remember. Other things, like more bolts. Didn't take long, though."

"How about Luis or Felix?" Ben asked.

"Felix don't let Luis drive the truck," Alberto said. "Had an accident once. Felix went to get bigger logs for the rail, though."

"Where?" Ben asked.

"We keep vigas and smaller logs over near the trash dump, near the Pot Creek ruin," Alberto said. "Luis and me, we stripped a bunch of them the day before."

Ben pushed himself up from the pickup. "Okay, amigo, thanks," he said. He heard his car phone. "Good luck with the distributor," he waved.

As he pulled out, he rang his office. "Ben," Pete Montoya said, "Horace Stern just called. You better get out there right away. They found the murder weapon."

"On my way," he said. He pulled out his flashing light, but left it on the seat. On his way to the fort a nagging thought ran through his mind. Something someone had said in his earlier interviews. He was sure it would come to him.

The highway was almost empty and he didn't need his light. He was there inside seven minutes.

◇◇◇

When Graciella had burst into the Commander's Quarters, Karen, Maria and Horace were sitting at the table, just beginning lunch. Catching her breath, Graciella had told them of her discovery. Horace had immediately gone back to the office and replaced the tool room padlock with a new one, then had called the police. Pete Montoya said he would send someone out immediately, and would notify Ben Sandoval.

By the time Ben arrived, Frank Collins had already retrieved the trowel and placed it in a plastic bag. In another, he had put the rag that had covered it. All were standing at the office door when Ben walked in.

Frank showed him the trowel, which Graciella had positively identified as hers. "We'll run chemistry for blood traces, Ben," Frank said. "From its size and shape, it could easily have been the murder weapon."

Ben turned to Horace. "Who has access to the tool room?" he asked.

"Felix and I have the only keys, Lieutenant," Horace said. "However, it is frequently left unlocked during the day. Especially when the men are working with heavy tools."

"Luis and Alberto don't have keys?"

"No," Horace said. "We've had thefts in the past. We want to keep access to a minimum."

"Only works when it's locked," Ben said. "You or Ms. Brown recollect if it was open Wednesday afternoon?"

Karen said, "It probably was, Lieutenant. I can't recall." She thought a moment. "Alberto was in and out a few times. Maybe the others as well."

"I'll have a talk with Felix," Ben said. "Meanwhile, keep the new padlock on. I'll want to give the room an inspection."

"Ben, Felix is in Santa Fe today," Graciella said. "That's why Danny helped Greg at the site."

Ben looked at his watch. One-fifteen. "I'll check his place," Ben said. "If his wife is home she can tell me when he'll be back." He and Collins walked to the courtyard exit. "Frank, I'll want your results as soon as you have them."

Graciella turned to Horace. "I almost forgot, Dr. Stern. Greg wants a vehicle barricade put up on the site road. He asked me if you could have Felix do it sometime today." She told them about her visit with Joseph Espinosa. "As far as I'm concerned," she said, "that kiva can sit there until this thing is over. I won't go near it alone."

Then she remembered what she had promised Greg. "Oh, I've got to get flagging tape for the site," she said. "I'll get Ben to take me over."

"I'll tell Felix when I see him, Grace," Horace said.

Graciella went to the archeology lab. She got a roll of florescent orange tape and six fourteen-inch steel chaining pins. Used in surveying, these were about a foot long, sharp at one end with an eye on the other. As she locked the lab, Ben approached from Felix's house across the gravel road.

"Graciella," he called. "Can you come with me for a minute?"

"Ben, I need you to go with me to the site," she said.

"That's exactly where we're going," he smiled. They walked up to the fort where he was parked. "What are those?"

"I need to put flagging around the top of the kiva, remember? What did you want?"

He explained as they drove out. "Felix's wife expects him before dinner," Ben said. "Around five o'clock. I want you to show me where the trash dump is. Alberto says they keep logs and vigas there for repairs."

The crossed the bridge over Pot Creek. About a hundred yards up the rise, the deeply rutted dirt road curved to the right, heading east. At the curve, a second road continued north to the site, which was some two hundred yards beyond. Graciella directed Ben to the right. The road continued another three hundred yards, then turned north for another hundred.

A large sanitary landfill had been dug in a clearing, plastic bags and other debris scattered at the near end of the depression. Ben stopped and they got out. To the left of the landfill were cleaned timbers of various lengths, stacked off the ground on railroad ties. A few were three to four inches in diameter, suitable for *latillas* and bridge rails.

"You ever hear the men working here?" Ben asked. He climbed up on the logs, visualizing where the site was. Probably a couple of hundred yards, maybe more, to the northwest. The same pinyon-juniper scrub that separated the site from the Forest Service nature trail was present here.

"Not that I can recall," Graciella said. "Why?"

Ben looked at the trash dump. "How often do they bring trash here?"

"Every morning," Graciella said. "Early. It's the first thing they do."

"How early?"

"Usually, when I'm getting up, the men come by each apartment to empty the trash," she said. "Seven or seven-thirty. They load it into the pickup and dump it."

Ben stood on the log pile a few minutes looking around. Then he jumped down and they drove to Pot Creek.

Graciella pushed the chaining pins into the soft backfill around the top of the kiva. Then she tied the flagging tape to one and passed it through the holes of the others, finally tying it to the original pin. A bright florescent hexagon now defined a no-walk zone over the kiva.

"Ben," she said, "give me just a minute here, okay?" She stepped down the ladder and stood on the kiva floor. Amazing how pristine the condition is, she thought. A low adobe bench encircled the floor except for the opening of the ventilator shaft. No other kivas—or pithouses—in this northern district had benches. Only those at Chaco and in parts of the Jemez. She walked over to the wall and inspected it. Around parts of it remnants of adobe plaster were still clinging to the coarser adobe construction. Almost a *tierra blanca*, she noted. Had it been painted? She looked closely, but could see no trace of pigment. A patch of floor west of the firepit was in direct sunlight, and she knelt down, inspecting it for any trace of a burned line. None. Silly, she thought, this kiva and the one in the vision were obviously different. She looked to the right of the firepit, following an imaginary line to the south wall. There! Next to the wall, three charred kernels! This is an obvious coincidence, she told herself. She moved to the left of the firepit. Another kernel, then another, next to the firepit. She moved to the north wall. Four, five more, all charred! All along a single line!

She now scanned the rest of the floor carefully. Nowhere did she find any evidence of burning. Only the firepit, and the partially-filled ashpit next to it. She sat back on her heels for a moment, her thoughts running back over the details. There was no altar here, no other feature on the floor except the deflector between firepit and ashpit. And the ventilator damper. She moved to the ventilator. A sandstone slab, shaped to overlap the opening, rested firmly against it. She examined it closely, running her fingers along its perimeter. It had been sealed with adobe. Sealed! Dampers were never sealed shut! They were moved each time a fire was set. They must have sealed this, knowing it would no longer be used, when they vacated the kiva.

But why had it been left intact? If abandoned, why not filled in? She looked again at the ventilator. If abandoned, why *sealed*? She touched it again. To seal something *inside*?

I've got to know, she said to herself. She reached in her pocket and took out her penknife, opened the larger blade, began cutting along the adobe seal. She cut enough away to expose about six inches of the stone's edge. She pressed her fingers on the edge and pulled towards her. Not enough purchase here. She cut deeper, into the wall, creating a small space for two or three fingers to reach slightly behind the thin stone slab. She wedged her fingers in and carefully pulled.

The stone loosened, broke the seal, and separated from the wall. With it, a musty odor seeped outward. An earthy smell, of mushrooms and mildew and something not familiar, slightly pungent, began to fill the kiva chamber. Graciella sneezed.

Behind the stone, darkness. Graciella leaned the stone against the wall next to the opening. The horizontal shaft, some eighteen inches high and over a foot wide, was clear of debris. Except something along the bottom. "Ben," Graciella called up to him, "do you have a flashlight?"

Ben leaned down and peered in. "What are you doing, Graciella?"

"A flashlight, Ben," she said. "Please!"

A minute later, he climbed down the ladder with the flashlight from his pickup. Graciella directed the beam along the floor of the shaft. The foot bones lay about eight inches inside. Beyond them, the left and right tibia and fibula, then the femora and, its position face down, a still-articulated pelvis. The upper limb bones lay alongside the collapsed rib cage, the thoracic and lumbar vertebrae resting in a disarticulated line in the center. She moved the beam beyond them, to the end of the tunnel about eight feet in. There, where the vertical shaft to the surface had been, was another sandstone slab, sealing off the end of the tunnel. Along the ceiling of the ventilator was a row of small *latillas*, two to three inches in diameter and spaced the same distance apart, over which appeared to have been laid a woven mat to seal the tunnel roof.

Graciella played the beam again toward the back of the floor. She could make out the two scapulae—the shoulder blades—and some smaller, cervical vertebrae. Immediately beyond these was a small, intact inverted pot. Where the skull should have been.

"Ben," Graciella said, "do you see. . . ." her voice trailed off.

"Yes," Ben said. "The skull is missing."

Graciella sneezed again.

19

It was 3:15 when Graciella and Ben returned to the fort. Graciella had carefully removed the pelvis—both innominates and the sacrum. She had then positioned her knees between the leg bones and one elbow where the pelvis had been, in order to remove the pot. The flashlight revealed no other grave goods. Before leaving, they had re-positioned the damper, using a smaller slab they found outside to help hold it in place.

She, Ben, Ned, and Horace now sat in the archeology lab examining the recovered items. Graciella's excitement had drawn their attention particularly to the pot and the feather that lay beneath it. The pot, actually a small bowl, was buff-slipped. On its exterior rim was a red band with negative design in the form of small buff dots, the buff being the underlying slip. On the interior bottom was a black-painted figure, its form so stylized as to obscure the nature of whatever animal or human it represented. It was certainly not a pueblo bowl, Graciella had said, at least not of a type she had ever seen. Its shape and interior design were reminiscent of Mimbres pottery in southern New Mexico. Perhaps Greg could identify it.

The feather was from a parrot. Scarlet Macaw, to be exact, Horace had said. These were favored for decoration and ceremonies in many parts of Mexico, where Horace had done some ethnolinguistic work.

With the pelvis, Graciella was more certain. It was definitely female, she could tell, from the broad angle of the sciatic notch of the ilium. The pubic symphysis would indicate the approximate age, once it had been compared with age-standards developed for osteological interpretation. Had the skull and teeth been present, aging the skeleton would have been easier, but the recovered arm and leg bones should help.

As they speculated on these items, Maria came in. "Lieutenant, Luis and Jorgé Lujan are here," she said. "Greg's not back yet. Can you and Graciella show them to the site?"

Graciella looked up at Ben. "Yes," she said. She was very uneasy about leaving them there unsupervised. "Ben, we've got more to do there," she said. "Measurements, detailed studies. . . ."

"Let's talk to them, Graciella," he said. "We'll make sure they won't disturb anything."

They followed Maria up to the office, where she introduced them. Luis was a young man of about twenty-three, slightly built and clean shaven, with straight black hair that fell just below the ears. His broad, thin mouth was framed by a square chin. Jorgé was a few years younger, probably nineteen. His features resembled his brother's, with a smaller, pouting mouth. His dark hair reached his shoulders and was parted in the middle. Both wore jeans and white, long-sleeved shirts buttoned at the collar. Luis wore a single strand of turquoise beads.

"I'm so very sorry about your sister," Graciella looked at them sympathetically.

Luis gave her a solemn look. "Thank you," he said.

"I will help you any way I can," Graciella said. "Can you tell me what you need to do at the site?"

"We must do some prayers for her," Luis said. "Where she died." He looked at his brother. "We will spend the night there." He paused, then said to Ben and Graciella. "But we will not do any harm to the place. When we see the place, I can tell you more."

"You can follow us over," Ben said. "We'll show you where to park." He turned to Graciella. "I need to speak with Luis and Jorgé first, privately. Won't take long." He said to Luis, "Just a few questions for the investigation."

Graciella showed them into the Library, then went back to the lab to secure the artifacts and pelvis in a cabinet. The others had left. She wrote a brief note for Greg, which she took to his apartment and slid into the door frame just above the knob. When she returned to the compound, Ben and the Lujan brothers were just finishing.

Ben and Graciella drove over in the Bronco, with Luis and Jorgé following in an old black Mustang. They parked next to each other and walked up to the excavation. Where Anita had died was directly over the opening to the kiva, Ben indicated, and the four of them went down the ladder.

"Luis," Ben said, "we believe that Anita was killed while she was preparing to do some ritual here. We found a feather in the firepit, which must have fallen in."

Luis and Jorgé looked around the kiva, then at each other. "Yes," Luis said, "Antonio told us." Jorgé had remained silent from the beginning, and it was apparent that his brother would do all of the talking. It was also apparent that both of them were uneasy about being here. Whatever they have to do, Graciella thought, was probably something they had never done before.

"My brother and I will spend the night down here," Luis said, "but we will not disturb your excavation." He climbed the ladder, the others following. On top, he stood and looked around the site, at the overgrown mounds of backfilled rooms and unexcavated units. "You must trust us," he said to Graciella, "and you must promise not to allow anyone to visit." He gave her an intense, almost pleading look. "Please understand me. What we do here is not anything secret. But it is Indian. We have made preparations, back at the pueblo, for her safe journey. Purifications, you would call them."

He paused, thinking his way to an explanation. "These preparations continue for four days at our home. But our sister was murdered here, and her death is not yet complete. We will help her to complete it here." He looked down into the kiva. "This is the fourth day," he said softly.

They all stood silently. "No one will disturb you," Ben said after a moment.

"We are putting up a barricade at the entrance to this road," Graciella said. "When you leave, you can move the barricade and then replace it. When will you finish?"

"At dawn," Luis said. He and Jorgé went to the Mustang while Ben and Graciella stood waiting. They returned with bed rolls and two small paper bags. They set the bedrolls down. Luis turned to Ben and Graciella. "We will build no fire," he said. "Only a single candle." He reached out his hand to them. "Thank you," he said.

Ben and Graciella left them and drove back to the fort. It was four-thirty, and Felix had not yet returned. She would have to remember to get that barricade up before nightfall, Graciella thought. She felt heartbreak for the two boys, together in the kiva. Such a desperately lonely vigil.

Ben left, promising to return around six-thirty. They would all meet at Horace and Maria's.

Graciella went to her apartment to wash up for dinner, then checked Greg's apartment. The note was gone, but Greg was not there.

She found him in the lab, the pot and feather on the table. He was leafing through a book as she entered. "Grace," he said, "this is fantastic! Do you know what this is?"

"It's not Anasazi," Graciella said. "Trade ware. Do you know?"

He held up the bowl. "I can't be certain," he said with excitement, "but it's got an Aztec design!"

"Aztec!" Graciella exclaimed.

"Well, not actually Aztec, Grace," Greg said, "but here, look at this figure in the bottom. That's a feathered serpent! I'll swear to it." He sat back. "You know, Grace, this bowl has features which tie it to many places. It's overall design is quite similar to those from Casas Grandes, in northern Chihuahua, and the interior design location, and the vessel form, are like Mimbres, in the Mogollon Rim area where I worked."

Greg pointed again to the design. "But the motif! This is Mesoamerican! Grace, I believe this bowl was an heirloom brought here from far to the south. It's unbelievable!" He leafed through one of the texts next to him on the table. "I'll have to look back through some of these reports," he said. "I know Mesoamerican motifs crop up in many places in the Southwest, southern Arizona, Pueblo Bonito at Chaco. But I know of none this far north."

"How about the feather, Greg?" Graciella asked. "Horace said it's a Macaw."

He held up the feather. "Parrot feathers were widespread in northern Mexico," he said. "In fact, Macaws were actually raised in postclassic times, along the Western Sierras. They traded them from Sinaloa north, probably to southern Arizona, at least."

Graciella examined the bowl again. It was very little worn, as if used only occasionally. Its surfaces had a smooth satin finish, even slightly glossy in places. "Can you estimate a date for this?" she asked.

"Only by inference," Greg replied. "It's likely Late Postclassic in Mexican terms. Mid-Fourteenth Century." He realized the implications. "By God," he said, "it was almost certainly brought here just at the end of the Pot Creek occupation! No later than 1350 A.D."

Graciella asked, nervously, "Traded in, do you think, or brought in by the culture that made it?"

Greg looked at her curiously. "Traded, of course!" he said. "Brought by its makers? Grace, think! If it represented a migration from the south, where did they go? Where is the other evidence of their presence?"

Perhaps, Graciella thought but did not say it, if the migrant group had been a small clan, under a powerful leader, seeking refuge in the less populated northern reaches of the Rio Grande. . . .

"I'll do some reading," Greg said, searching out a book from the stack. "Maybe I can pin this down."

Graciella looked at her watch. It was after five and Graciella realized that she never ate the lunch Maria had prepared. "Greg, let's go eat and talk about this," she said.

He waved her off, selecting a volume from the Casas Grandes report. "You go ahead, Grace," he said. "I'll be along."

As she rose to leave, she said, "By the way, Greg, Lieutenant Sandoval wants to see us all after dinner, at Maria and Horace's place."

She left the lab and walked slowly across the Parade Ground, thinking. She turned before entering her apartment, listening. From beyond the fort, across the highway, over the pinyon-juniper scrub, she caught the faint staccato notes. Moving in and out of audible range, carried on some ephemeral draft, came the haunting music of an Indian flute.

The soft lament, though filled with melancholy, gave her a feeling of peacefulness. Or did her change in mood come from a growing awareness that the links between her two realities were becoming stronger?

Her fear of personal danger had begun to ebb. *They* will protect me, she thought, lightly. She decided to take the nature trail to the Dining Hall.

20

Ben sat at his desk, going over his notes from the Lujan interview. Luis had been straightforward with him, Ben thought. It was good that Ben had the confidence of Antonio Romero. Tony had encouraged the two of them to provide whatever information Ben sought. Jorgé, the quiet one, had said little. It appeared that he had indeed known little about his sister's involvement with the ancient Taos traditions. He appeared to be interested only in finding out who her murderer was, but neither one could suggest a possible suspect.

Luis, on the other hand, was more sympathetic to Anita's efforts to discover hidden secrets of their heritage. She had from time to time confided in him, and shared her frustration in dissecting truth from fable.

Her family had not missed her the night after she was murdered, thinking she had spent the night at Picuris, as she occasionally did.

She had visited Picuris several times in the past year, Luis said, speaking mainly with the elder Joseph Espinosa and, until her death in early Spring, Joseph's older sister, Reina. She had established a close relationship with Reina—whose affiliation with the Sky Kiva had given her the name *Páxia*, "Flower-Waiting"—and she was the one who had told Anita about the legendary North-Side Kiva.

As an adolescent, Reina had been told by her grandmother about ceremonies in the scalp house, *p'exayna*, to rid the pueblo of *cahane*—witches who sought to do harm. A particular witch from the past had been chief of the North Side Kiva in their earlier village, and had transformed into a young girl during some critical ceremony. As a result, the mountain spirits of their ancestors had become angry and destroyed the village. The survivors had settled at Picuris and Taos, the original North Side clan members being the Picuris ancestors.

The enmity between the two pueblos had disappeared over the years, except for the occasional mischief caused by this witch. Reina had been told about the ceremony—she had never witnessed it—and folklore had it that only if it were performed in the original kiva would they be rid of this evil spirit.

Luis said that Anita had convinced Reina to ask the elders about the ritual itself, and that shortly before her death Reina had recited it to Anita. Anita had been excited, Luis said, and had sworn Luis to secrecy. There was someone at Picuris, not a spirit, intent on preventing such a ceremony. No, Anita had not known who. Or why.

After Reina had died, Luis said, Anita had apparently felt some sense of urgency. After that, his sister had become somewhat remote and preoccupied, and had not spoken to him about the ritual. Nor had she mentioned Pot Creek, although she had spent more time volunteering at the Forest Service Cultural Site.

Luis did not know what had caused Reina's death. Natural causes, he supposed. She had been in her eighties.

Frank Collins came in as Ben finished reviewing his notes. "This is the one, Ben," Frank said, holding the trowel. "Traces of blood, AB-positive, on the blade. Not a common bloodtype. Less than five percent of the population has it."

"But Anita did?" Ben asked.

"She did, indeed." Frank put the trowel on the desk, with its identifying tag attached. "We had less luck with prints, though." He clicked his tongue. "Just a smudge from a thumb on the metal haft. The way a trowel is held, you wouldn't get more than a thumb print anyway."

"Any blood on the rag, Frank?"

"None at all. It's just a greasy rag."

Ben put the trowel aside. "Thanks, Frank," he said. He put his report on the Lujan interview in the file folder and closed it. Then he opened his desk and pulled out the sheet of paper on which he had earlier defined the "Motive" and "Opportunity" columns. He studied it for several minutes, then marked through all the names except three: Luis Garza, Alberto Sanistevan, and Felix Mondragon. To these he added a fourth: Joe Espinosa.

He leaned back in his chair and put his feet up on the desk. He reached over and picked up the trowel, touching its sharpened edge to his finger, and closed his eyes. All four had opportunity, he thought. Their exact whereabouts at the time of the murder—sometime between, say, 3:15 and 4:00—could not be established. Joe Espinosa was presumably back at Picuris then, but Ben had not checked to see if anyone could corroborate this. The other three were working together, but made trips to get supplies. Even Luis Garza could have taken his own car, which had been parked in the lot by the footbridge, over to the site.

But if any of the three had done this, they would have had to know precisely when Anita was going to be there. None of them had been absent from the bridge very long. Not long enough to be laying in wait for Anita. Only Espinosa could have done this, had he known she was there. He was missing something, Ben said to himself. Turn it around, look for the other angle.

Okay, no one was there waiting for her. No one knew she was going to Pot Creek. Her car wasn't even there. Ben sat up. Her car! Someone driving from town could have seen her car at the Cultural Site. Even though inside the entrance, it was parked in clear view of the highway. Joe Espinosa? Do the scenario, Ben thought. Espinosa drove to the Cultural Site, saw her car, parked next to her. Found no one, surmised she was at the excavation. Approached the site from the scrub forest, came upon her. Argued? Attempted to assault her sexually? Killed her with Graciella's trowel, which with the pick had fallen onto the collapsed debris, left the way he had come.

Then how did the trowel wind up in the tool shed? Ben struck through the name. Too convoluted, unless he and his brother-in-law conspired together, and Alberto placed the trowel as a miscue to the investigation. If that were the case, the trowel would have been more conspicuous. Joe Espinosa, you're released, Ben told himself.

Ben leaned back again. He still didn't have the angle. "Alright, Apache," he said out loud. "You're overlooking the obvious." He picked up the paper. The motive column was blank. Find the motive, find the murderer, he repeated to himself. From old man Sandoval, from Graciella, and now from Luis Lujan, a motive kept repeating. Ritual. Prevention of same. Fear of conjuring evil spirits. Witchcraft. Superstition, this belief in witches, Ben thought. But most pueblos carry it deep in tradition.

He put the paper on his desk and stood up. How is the belief in witches different from a vision quest? As a fourteen-year-old, his quest had been serious, if half-hearted. How long had it been since he quit believing in his golden eagle, his guardian spirit? *Had* he quit believing? The things he told Graciella on U.S. Hill: Reality is all around us, but recognition comes in bits and fragments. Did he believe that?

He paced his office. Belief *is* reality. Fear of the unknown is powerful, he thought to himself, but fear of the *known*, especially if that known lies beyond the so-called natural world of most of us, is more powerful still. Especially if the fear is focused on a special place.

They are legion, he thought, these places of power. Where the spirits can heal—or destroy. Stonehenge, the spring at Lourdes, even here in New Mexico in the miraculous soil at Chimayo. And the kiva at Pot Creek? He continued pacing. Portals to the other side, either gateways to Heaven or across the Styx to Hell.

Say someone truly believes—*knows*—that this one kiva has a special, ancient significance. That it harbors the evil to bring havoc, even death, to the living. That a forgotten ceremony, intentionally mis-performed there, destroyed a community. A once-forgotten ceremony. Suppose someone knew that the ceremony was now in the hands of one who could perform it again, and that the one, single, critical place to perform it was being excavated. Would the convergence of these two facts, the rediscovered ritual and the excavated kiva, bring a special fear? Would the knowledge that the inertia of history was rapidly bringing them to closure be sufficient motive for murder? At any cost?

"Of course it would!" Ben said aloud.

Pete Montoya stuck his head in the door. "You arguing with yourself, Ben?" Pete asked. "I think you work too hard, man."

"It's an Indian thing, Pete," Ben laughed. "I need you to make a call for me. To Picuris. Important." He wrote out a long note on his pad and handed it to Pete. He looked at his watch. Just after six. "I'm going to be late. Reach me at the number I wrote down. I'll be at the fort." He put his folder in the top drawer of his desk and turned out the light. "You mind?"

"Hell, man, it's only Saturday night," Pete grinned. "What else I got to do? I can always go dancin' *next* month, right?" He followed Ben to the door. "You close to findin' the guy, Ben?"

"I'm always close, amigo," Ben slapped him on the shoulder. "Keep trying until you get that information. Then call me, Pete."

On the drive to the fort, Ben went over the new scenario in his mind. The motive all along was simply to prevent the likelihood of that ceremony ever being performed. That meant either preventing the excavation of the kiva or preventing the person with knowledge of the ritual procedure from performing it. Or both.

That meant that the opportunity column had to be restricted to those who could have been at the site on three particular occasions: to fill in Graciella's excavation last Monday evening, to be present as the excavation collapsed on her Wednesday morning, and to be there again Wednesday afternoon.

Still left the same suspects, Ben thought, except for motive. Who could have known about Anita's interest in the kiva? And in learning the ceremony? Someone at Picuris, or close to the Espinosa family. Joe and Alberto.

It's unlikely that Joe would not have known about Anita's interest. He worked with her at the Cultural Site, certainly knew of her visits to his parents at Picuris. He could have filled in the site on Monday evening, was admittedly at the Cultural Site early Wednesday morning when Anita was at Pot Creek, and returned there later that morning. Where was he at four o'clock? Even hiding the trowel would have been feasible—the tool room was left unlocked from time to time. Even the day after, Thursday, he could have come in at noon when the office was locked, seeking a place to hide it and finding by chance the ideal location.

Alberto worked at the fort, had ample opportunity to visit the site Monday evening without arousing suspicion. He wasn't home early Wednesday when Joe arrived with the firewood. Instead of getting gas, as he claimed, he could have been at the trash dump early, his truck hidden there.

He could even have known that Graciella was spending the night there and been waiting when she began the digging that led to the collapse. Seen, perhaps, by Anita as he was prepared to prevent the excavation, he could have returned to his truck and left after Maria had taken Graciella to Holy Cross. That would have put him back at his house by, say, 8:30—not 8:00 as he had claimed.

Felix, likewise, had all of the opportunities—probably more than the others—and his whereabouts could easily be covered. He alone had a key to the tool room, as well. But what about motive? He would be unlikely to know about Anita's plans, much less her schedule. He obviously cared for Graciella's welfare, and had little sympathy for the superstitions of his workers regarding the site. What would he have to gain? Nevertheless. . . .

Luis, Ben thought, was probably the least likely of the four, simply because of lack of opportunity on Wednesday afternoon. It would have been simply too risky to drive his own vehicle to the site to commit murder, even had he known about Anita's knowledge of the ritual.

As he pulled into the fort, the nagging thought again struck Ben. I'm missing something obvious, he said to himself. But when he had reviewed all of his notes from the many interviews, nothing had struck him.

Felix's truck was at his house, and Ben decided to stop there first. His adobe house was set back off the gravel road to the left, across from the fort compound. The backhoe, tractor, and two riding mowers were parked in the large yard to the left of the house. Near the front of the yard was a fuel tank raised on a metal frame, and Felix's truck was parked next to it. He was filling his tank when Ben approached.

"Good evening, Lieutenant," Felix said.

"Evening, Felix," Ben said. "How was Santa Fe?"

"Very hot," Felix said, "and crowded. I don't like to go there anymore, but we needed supplies. I just got back. You care to join us for dinner?"

"No, thanks," Ben said. "I won't keep you. I'm on my way to see the Sterns. Had a few questions for you, Felix."

"Sure, Lieutenant. How can I help you?"

"On Wednesday, Felix, Alberto was late to work. Is that right?" Ben asked.

"That's right. I gave him permission." Felix looked up from fueling. "He was getting some firewood."

"You remember what time he arrived?" Ben asked.

"I guess close to ten, maybe 9:30," Felix said. "No earlier than that. Luis and me, we needed three people to set the vigas for the bridge, so we had to wait."

"Did Alberto go back to the fort during the afternoon, Felix?" Ben asked. "For some supplies, maybe?"

"Yeah, maybe a couple times. I sent him for an extension cord, I remember." Felix finished fueling and replaced the hose on its hook at the tank. "And he went across for a bridge rail."

Ben looked up in surprise. "Alberto did?" he asked. "I thought you brought the rails."

"I did," Felix said, screwing the cap on his tank. "But one of them was too short. I sent him back for another."

"Felix, you remember when that was?"

"You mean what time?" Felix asked. "Let's see, it was late afternoon. Maybe four o'clock."

Ben considered this new information, revising the scenario in his mind. "Felix, how well do you know Joe Espinosa?"

"Joe? I don't know him that well," Felix said. "Guess I run into him now and then. Why?"

"I was just wondering if he ever comes over here. When he's working across the road."

"A few times, maybe," Felix said. "To have lunch with Alberto. Don't think I've seen him lately, though."

"Okay, Felix, thanks for your time," Ben shook his hand. "Go get some dinner."

Ben backed out and drove around to the Commander's Quarters. It was six-forty, and he didn't figure he'd be staying long. Just until he received the call from Pete.

21

At six-twenty, Graciella was just finishing dinner with Ned, Danny and Andy. She had told them about Greg's identification of the bowl, and his determination to find its probable source. Knowing him, Graciella had laughed, he'll still be in the lab at sunrise, searching the literature.

The four of them left, Graciella riding with Ned. When they arrived at Horace and Maria's, Karen was already there. Maria had set out some chips, cheese, and bread. A full wine carafe was on the table. "Might as well have refreshments," Maria said, "since this is a command performance for us."

As Graciella poured a glass of wine, Greg came in the back door, a broad smile on his face. "I've got it!" he said. "I know where the bowl came from!" He spied the cheese and bread and headed for it. "Food," he said, brightly. "Thanks, Maria. Guess I missed dinner."

"Okay, Greg," Graciella said. "Tell us."

"All of you sit," Greg said, filling a plate. "This is going to be a short lesson in prehistory." He pulled up a chair.

When the Toltec Empire fell in the mid-12th Century, Greg explained, their influence in Western Mexico began to wane. The expanding Aztecs had concentrated mainly on the eastern and southern regions. During the century that followed, various cycles of conquest and defeat characterized the Aztec, as a series of rulers established alliances and advanced the cult of human sacrifice.

In this maneuvering for power among kinship groups, deposed leaders often sought new alliances outside the immediate sphere of influence. In coastal Sinaloa, somewhere around 1200 A.D., there was a rather sudden influx of Aztec influence, so pervasive as to suggest an actual migration. This reached its height by about 1300 A.D., in the Guasave Phase, characterized by strong ceremonialism and stylized art motifs—including the plumed serpent, representing Quetzalcoatl.

This influence expanded northward, following both a coastal route and the corridor just east of the mountains, into Chihuahua. Elements are found in the Tardio Period at Casas Grandes, just south of the border, by 1300 A.D.

This period, from 1200 to 1300 A.D., Greg explained, was the very time of native upheaval and movement in the northern southwest. Pueblo culture expanded into the Mogollon region and Chaco and Mesa Verde were abandoned. Furthermore, it was around 1300 A.D. when the pueblo ceremonialism we know today began—the kachina cult, prayer sticks, masked dances. New ceramic styles were introduced—including the motif of the plumed serpent. One such motif is even known in Rio Grande Glaze Ware ceramics in the mid-14th Century.

This bowl, Greg said, was almost certainly from Guasave. Whether traded here or brought, it represented definite Mesoamerican influence. Sinaloa was likewise a major source for Macaw feathers. The two most probably arrived together, and not long before Pot Creek abandonment.

"Greg, I think it was brought here," Graciella said. "We know that Taos and Picuris Pueblos are the only ones in the Rio Grande without masked dances, and the kachina cult supposedy never reached here. Neither is there clan organization." She brought more wine for herself and Greg. "Yet, we also know that after 1250 A.D., the cult was known here, and probably practiced." She reminded him of the single pottery fragment, dating late in the Pot Creek occupation, which showed a masked and horned kachina figure. The motif was, furthermore, from inside a bowl in the center—a decorative zone never before nor since used on ceramics in the region.

"We'll never know, Grace," Greg said. "But it's certainly a possibility."

"And this migrant group, the last to join the pueblo, caused its downfall," Graciella said. Greg looked at her in surprise.

"That's what the Picuris legend says," Ben Sandoval interjected. He had entered while Graciella had been speaking, and had stood quietly back, listening. Everyone turned to him. "Let me tell you what I learned today," he said. He told them what Luis Lujan had said about his sister, and Reina, and the ceremony. "I'm convinced," he said, "that Anita was murdered by someone who wanted to destroy the kiva and prevent the ceremony."

He let the shock of this revelation sink in while he cut a slice of cheese.

He wanted them all to think along these lines before he asked them any questions.

Andy was the first to speak. "Lieutenant," she asked, "is that why Joseph Espinosa came to me to warn Grace? Does he know who killed Anita?"

"I think he probably does, Miss Abbott," Ben said. "But he'll never say. You don't mention the name of a witch."

"You obviously don't know, either, Lieutenant," Horace said, "or you wouldn't be here. You need information we can provide, correct?"

Ben gave him a slight smile. "Incisive and to the point, Dr. Stern," he said. "I have my suspicions, of course. But I do have a few questions."

"Go ahead," Maria said. "And have some wine, too."

"Thanks, I'll pass on the wine," Ben said. "Perhaps some water?"

She went to get it and Ben moved closer to the group. "Most of you know the two men who work with Felix," he said. "Alberto and Luis. If any of you recall their whereabouts during the day last Wednesday, either early morning or afternoon, I'd like to know." He paused. "Please don't second guess me on them," he said. "It's not that they are suspects. I'm only trying to corroborate their own recollections. The more people I can eliminate, the better."

"They were outside my apartment early," said Ned. "Felix and one of the men. About seven o'clock they picked up the trash."

"Yes," said Karen. "Felix picked up the trash at the chalet about seven-fifteen or so. I was getting dressed."

"Was anyone with him?" asked Ben.

"I don't know," Karen answered. "There may have been someone in the truck, but I didn't look."

Maria brought Ben a glass of water. "I was at the art building across the road then," she said. "I saw the truck pass, but didn't notice who was in it. That time is about right."

Ben turned to Maria. "What time did you go over there?"

"Just about then," she said. "I had just left my car to enter the building."

Ben turned to the group. "Did any of you in the chalet, or you, Maria, see any other vehicle come through. Around that time, or earlier?"

They all shook their heads. Karen and Andy had been in their showers around seven. Danny had got up around seven to make coffee. "Wait," Danny said. "I remember Grace driving to the site sometime after seven. Shortly after, I heard another vehicle pass." He thought a moment. "Could have been the pickup with the trash, but this would have been around 7:30."

None of the others recalled hearing a vehicle. Ben asked whether anyone knew Joe Espinosa, whom he described. No one did. As they exchanged comments among themselves, the telephone rang. The call was for Ben and he moved towards the kitchen to talk. When he finished, his expression had changed.

"Well, folks, you can relax," he said. "I believe we've narrowed the field to one. I have to leave."

"Who is it, Ben?" Graciella asked, eagerly.

"I'll tell you after the arrest, Graciella," Ben said. "But rest easy." He waved, "You folks enjoy your wine and cheese."

◇◇◇

Ben drove at normal speed, without using his light. He had told Pete Montoya to meet him at Alberto's house with another officer, and to bring the trowel.

Pete had called Picuris about the death of Reina Espinosa. She had died in early June. The death certificate had listed natural causes, but upon pressing the Governor, whom Pete knew, he had been told that the family was convinced it was a witch murder. The Governor himself firmly believed she had been murdered, by suffocation, while she was alone in the family adobe. Her nephew Joe had urged the Governor to seek a police investigation, but the family had resisted this. The Council had agreed to let it pass, not wishing to involve outsiders in pueblo business.

Joe would not have murdered his aunt and then called for an investigation. Furthermore, Joe had been with the Governor all Wednesday afternoon. They had driven to Santa Fe to meet with the hotel manager there. Joe was no longer a suspect.

But the damning evidence was against Alberto. The Governor had said that, upon marrying Joe's sister, Alberto had consistently warned Reina and the elder Joseph against telling Anita anything about the ancient beliefs. He had become so frightened of witches that he had moved off the reservation to live in Ranchos. Ben looked at his watch. Seven-thirty. He expected Alberto to be home.

He was. Pete and the other officer had Alberto standing beside the police car, in handcuffs, when Ben pulled up. Alberto was gesturing with his head and shouting. His wife was standing beside him.

He looked at Ben wild-eyed. "What the hell you guys doin'?" he shouted. "Man, I ain't done nothin' wrong!"

Ben indicated for the other officer to take Ms. Sanistevan inside. She was in tears and terrified. Then he turned to Alberto. "Alberto, you're being arrested on suspicion of the murder of Anita Lujan," he said. He recited Alberto's Miranda rights, and cautioned him to contact an attorney before saying anything.

"Don't need no goddamn *abogado*," Alberto said harshly. "I didn't kill no one!" He gave Ben a pathetic look. "I won't go *near* that old pueblo!" he said. "That girl. Wouldn't go near her, either! She was up to witchcraft!"

"Which is why you killed her," Ben said calmly, motioning for Pete to get the trowel. "With this," Ben said, taking the trowel.

"What?" Alberto stared at it, then looked back at Ben, then bent close to see the trowel better. "This. . .," Alberto sputtered, "this is. . .. Hey! You find this in the tool room at the fort?"

"Exactly where you put it, Alberto, after you used it on Anita," Ben said.

"You goddamn right I put it there!" Alberto looked at Pete, then Ben. "But I didn't kill no one with it! Hell, man, I found it Thursday morning in the trash pile! Figured it was one we use for layin' adobes, got picked up from the truck bed with the trash bags. Hell, man, all I did was carry it back!"

Ben looked at him intently. "Thursday. Who was with you, Alberto?"

"Jesus, I was by myself," Alberto pleaded. "Felix told me he had to haul the trash alone on Wednesday, I should do it alone on Thursday." His voice became weak as he realized he had no witnesses.

"You tell Felix or anyone about it?" Pete asked.

"Aw, man, I forgot all about it. Wasn't nothin' important." Alberto begged, "Jesus, you guys gotta believe me!"

Ben stood looking at him. He looked at the trowel in his hand. That nagging thought returned again, and this time he wouldn't let it go. The murderer came upon Anita, but not with intent to kill, not carrying a murder weapon. Argued. Struggled. Saw the pick and trowel Graciella had dropped. Picked up the trowel and. . . .

The pick! Something Felix said. When I interviewed him after the body was discovered. We talked about Graciella's accident. He said that it was lucky the wall didn't kill her—or "drive her pick into her when it fell". But how could he know she had the pick with her? And was using it? No one knew! Only Ned saw it when he went to retrieve her gear. And left it there because he couldn't reach it. And told no one. Felix wouldn't have known—unless he'd been there!

Felix had filled in the site Monday night. Had been there when the floor had collapsed beneath Graciella. Had been seen by Anita. And had returned to destroy the kiva when Anita came back!

Ben took Alberto by the shoulders. "I want you to tell me something, Alberto. Straight talk. You lie and you're a dead man. *Comprende?*"

"*Sí*, Lieutenant," Alberto gave Ben a look of desperation.

"What did Felix know about Anita? About the North Side Kiva? About the ceremony of the witch?" Ben held his shoulders tightly.

"He knew everything!" Alberto said. "Felix is Picuris, man. He grew up there! I talked to him about Anita's visits sometimes."

"He's Picuris?" Ben asked, incredulously.

"Not now, man," Alberto's voice shook. "He left the pueblo ten, twelve years ago. They kicked him out."

"Why?" Ben asked.

"He was against the ceremony they held at the Scalp House," Alberto replied. "Said it was bringing back evil spirits. He went crazy, man! Stole a fetish out of the Scalp House." Alberto sounded confident. "You ask my father-in-law. He had him thrown out!"

"Why haven't I heard about this?" Ben asked.

"Hey, they don't talk about it," Alberto said. "Besides, it was a long time ago. Felix, he's changed. He's okay, now."

"But he keeps to himself, you said," Ben released his grip. "Is he a witch, Alberto?"

"Jesus, man, you kiddin'?" Alberto moved his shoulders, trying to restore circulation. "Felix ain't no witch! I guess he'd kill one if he knew for sure. Jesus, I wouldn't work with no witch!"

Ben looked at Pete. Christ, he thought, it was right in front of me all along! "Let him go, Pete. You follow me to the fort. Hurry!"

Ben jumped into his truck, spun it around, and headed out with billows of dust behind him. He punched in the number for the Sterns. Maria answered. "Maria, this is Ben," he almost shouted. "Is Graciella still there?"

"No, Lieutenant," she said. "She's already left."

"Find her!" Ben said. "Keep her at your place. It's important. Tell her I'm on my way back there." He paused, not wanting to frighten her, then decided he had to. "And, Maria, tell her to stay away from Felix!"

He hung up before she could say anything. He pulled off the dirt road and onto the highway. This time, he plugged in his light and set it flashing on his roof.

Maria sat dumbfounded, the receiver still in her hand. She had wanted to tell him, that's exactly where Graciella was. At Felix's.

22

After Ben had left, the group sat in lively speculation over the person he had identified as the murderer. Who could it be? they wondered. Obviously, someone off the premises. "None of us, I can assure you," said Horace. He must be going after Alberto, Luis, or Joe Espinosa, Maria had said, since he had asked about no one else.

Graciella was the most relaxed and least curious. A heavy burden had been lifted, and she didn't care. She was safe. She drank another glass of wine and talked with Greg about the Aztec bowl.

Horace came over to join them. "Oh, Grace," he said. "I must apologize. I forgot to tell Felix to put up that barricade." He smiled. "Perhaps it's not necessary, now," he said.

Grace frowned. "Oh, I think we should put it up, Dr. Stern," she said. "I sort of promised the Lujan brothers." She looked at her watch. It was almost eight. This time of year, the sky would be dark within the hour.

"Look, I'll go tell Felix," she said. "It won't take a minute. Then I'll come back for some more of this delightful wine!" She was almost ebullient, partly due to the two glasses she'd already had.

The sky outside was turning a darker blue, although the tops of the hills to the east were still bathed in a golden light. Bright yellow and orange furrows of cloud hung just over the western ridge. It was going to be a beautiful sunset.

She knocked on Felix's door. When he answered, she said, "Felix, I hate to bother you this late. We need a barricade put up on the road to Pot Creek. I promised. Do you mind?"

He stepped outside. "Not at all, Miss Graciella," he said. "We've got one in my backyard I can use. Where should I put it?"

"Oh, I'll go with you, Felix," she said. "It's the least I can do, just to help."

"No need to do that," Felix smiled. "One person can handle it."

"I insist, Felix," she said. "Besides, I want to see the sunset."

They walked to the back yard. Behind the gasoline tank was a white-and-black striped barrier with two A-frame supports. They loaded them into Felix's truck.

As they drove out, Felix asked, "Miss Graciella, why do we need the barricade?"

"Oh, I guess you didn't know," Graciella said. "Anita Lujan's two brothers are spending the night at the site, and I promised no one would be allowed in."

Felix involuntarily slammed on the brakes. "I'm sorry," he quickly recovered. "Saw a rabbit in front of us." He drove on, crossing the highway. "Why are they there?" he asked.

"Some pueblo ritual for Anita," she said. "It has to be performed there. Where she was murdered. They're in the kiva."

"The kiva!" he turned to her. "No!" he said. "Miss Graciella, that's not right! You shouldn't let them!"

They crossed the Pot Creek bridge and began climbing. "Just there, Felix," Graciella said. "Where the road to the site begins." She turned to him, a little uneasy. "It's okay, Felix. Don't worry. They promised not to disturb anything." She touched his shoulder, knowing he was becoming upset. "Look, Felix, it's part of their religion. It's the least we can do, since she was killed here."

Felix parked heading into the road, just at the curve. He said nothing more. They both got out and unloaded the lumber. "The *Teotles*," he said beneath his breath. "They will bring back the *Xolotl*!" his voice was a low growl. "They must not!" His hands shook slightly as he put his end of the barricade into the slot of the A-frame.

"Felix?" Graciella said in a confused voice. The sky was darker blue now, with fingers of blood red and purple creeping along the western ridge beyond him.

"The *A-ten-calli* chiefs must be kept away from here!" Felix said in a deep, gruff voice, looking at her now. His black eyes glistened despite the waning light, piercing into her. She suddenly became cold and her fear returned. *Teotles*, he had said. The sacred ones. The priests. That's Nahuatl, she thought. Aztec! He had used that before, she now remembered! When she had been searching for shovels in the tool shed. How did he know Nahuatl? From her last journey into that other reality, she recalled the *A-ten-calli* people. The "Water-Side House"—in her vision it was the clan—of those who represented a danger to her people. How did he know *this*?

"First Reina, then Anita," Felix said, softly now, oblivious to Graciella's transfixed stare. "I stopped them from opening the way. I will stop others."

Oh, my God, she thought. Felix is the one! Ben doesn't know. He said he would protect me, and he doesn't know! She put her end of the barrier in A-frame, watching Felix carefully. "It's okay, Felix," she said in a voice that began to crack. She slowly backed up, using peripheral vision to look for an escape. She could run behind his truck, back towards the chalet, for help. No! she thought. Everyone is still at the party! The Lujan brothers were in the kiva. She would run there, at least have the mounds or the pinyon-juniper for cover.

"It's okay," she said again, moving towards the site. "Wait here. I've just got to check on. . . ." Her voice broke, and she turned and began running.

"No!" shouted Felix. "Come back, Graciella! I'll take you home."

She kept running. She looked back furtively, saw him moving in her direction, now breaking into a run. "Stop, Graciella!" he shouted. "You are in no danger! Come back!" She ran faster, already panting, the road before her stretching towards an ever-distant destination. Was he gaining? Oh, God, please don't fall, she told herself! Concentrate on the road.

Should she yell out? Lose some of her precious wind? She gave her head a quick turn, enough to catch a glimpse of Felix, still pursuing, gaining rapidly. The site lay fifty yards ahead. She wouldn't make it! The woods? He was too close for her to hide in the trees. It was now much darker. Darker still in the woods. "Luis!" she shouted. "Jorgé!"

She reached the clearing of the site. Just to the right, a dark shadow appeared. Their black Mustang! She looked back again. Felix was less than fifty feet behind her. Not enough time for her to open the door, scramble inside, shut and lock it. If it wasn't already locked! If the windows were up! Maybe she could keep the Mustang between them, long enough for Luis and Jorgé to help! "Luis!" she shouted again, as she reached the Mustang and quickly turned. She stopped in front of the hood, prepared to counter Felix's direction around the vehicle.

Felix continued toward the kiva, not stopping to seek her. Of course! The kiva was more important, now! Stopping the passage of *Xolotl*, Aztec dog of the underworld, was critical for him!

At the same instant, she saw Luis and Jorgé emerge from where the kiva was. The surface there was hidden by the intervening Unit VI, which Felix was now beginning to climb. As he passed, she heard his hard breathing. He had slowed, getting his bearings in the fading light.

"Luis!" Graciella shouted again. "He's coming toward you! He murdered Anita! Run!" She found herself following Felix up Unit VI. Something inside her compelled her, and even as she told herself she must escape, she continued. Felix was atop Unit VI, scanning the dark depression beyond which separated it from Unit VII. Graciella remembered a five-foot length of 2-by-2 lumber, used by an earlier excavation crew for securing plastic sheets, just this side of the mound summit. There! She saw it, just as Felix began a cautious but determined descent into the depression. She picked it up, climbing to the top of the mound, held it in both hands.

"Felix!" she shouted. He stopped and turned. At the same moment, Jorgé charged down the far side of the depression towards Felix.

"You bastard!" he shouted, lunging and catching Felix in the mid-section, both of them falling to the ground. Felix broke the hold of the younger man, rolled over on top of him, and sat up. With a single back-hand sweep he struck Jorgé in the face.

Graciella and Luis, from opposite sides, converged on Felix at this moment, Graciella a split second earlier. As she arrived, she swept the 2 X 2 in a wide arc, slamming it with force on Felix's neck.

Felix went suddenly down on his elbows, momentarily stunned. Christ, Graciella thought, that should have put him out! Before he could recover, Luis was on his back, attempting to get a strangle-hold on Felix's throat. Felix rose, almost, it appeared to Graciella, in slow motion, Luis on his back with what was now an effective hammer-lock around his neck, his feet locked around Felix's waist just above the heavy belly. Graciella then noticed that Luis was in Indian ceremonial costume, wearing only a breech-cloth and moccasins.

With a quickness which Graciella's senses could not immediately measure, Felix knelt down and surged upward and forward. Like some lifeless rag doll, Luis was ejected from his hold and was sent over Felix's head and against the lone juniper that grew in the depression. His limbs flailed as he cascaded off the branches and settled at the base, now only partially conscious.

A surge of adrenalin coursed through Graciella as she advanced. She swung the timber with good aim at the back of Felix's head. He turned in precise timing with her blow, as if knowing without seeing it, and grasped the piece at its apogee with one hand. As his arm continued the trajectory, he used and magnified her own force of muscle and sinew to pull the timber toward him. It rasped violently from her two hands, leaving torn flesh, and her inertia propelled her to him.

With a gutteral, unnatural howl, he grasped her shoulder with his left arm, casting the timber aside with his right. He pulled her with him as he ascended Unit VII, stood holding her at the entrance to the kiva. Graciella could see, behind him, the faint glow of the single candle, burning somewhere inside. He thrust her down, violently, to the mound's surface and released his hold, the kiva entrance behind and below him.

He glared down at her as she looked up. The last of the sun-reddened twilight gave his face an incendiary hue, made all the more sinister by the contorted smile on his face. "You are a foolish woman, Graciella!" he said in a voice approaching a sneer. "A disobedient, stupid child! I gave you all the warnings you should have needed." His voice, Graciella realized, was changing as he spoke. It was becoming stentorian, precise, articulate. It was no longer Felix.

"You were an innocent!" he bellowed. "Not even a messenger! Simply a convenient vehicle for this passage. You held one critical half, without knowing it. Anita Lujan," his anger spit the name out, "held the other, knowing it!" He knelt, and with one hand grasped her by the throat. "There are no more warnings, Graciella! You are no longer an innocent! It is time, once and forever, to close this gateway." He lifted her, painfully suspending her just beyond footreach of the surface. "You will join the others!"

As his hand grew tighter on her throat, Graciella felt herself slipping from consciousness. The intense pain below her jaw and the throbbing pressure against her carotid arteries was replaced by a tingling numbness, that last visitor of sensation before the final link to life is severed.

Then there was a sudden sense of transitory stoppage in the course of events, like a drain momentarily plugged, then released to disgorge its swollen contents. She felt a surge of power just within conscious range, then a flowing out, rapidly and forcefully. The grip on her throat was summarily released, and the sudden depressurization brought her back as she fell to the surface. Concurrently, Graciella felt an infiltration of strength—a deep force, well hidden—that quickly filled her body and reinforced her will. A scent of Juniper.

She opened her eyes and looked above. Hands on his hips and a defiant flare in his eyes, he bent forward, hovering over her. She raised herself on one elbow, and with her free hand open, fingers splayed, she thrust her palm upward against his jaw. A scent of sage.

Yelping in pain, Felix staggered backward, on the brink of the kiva wall. Graciella rose quietly. The look of utter dismay in his face fed her resolve. "You will never, never take me, you fragment of fetid dog," her words, in restrained anger, slithered from clenched teeth.

He quickly got to his feet. "Daughter of filth!" he said. "Return to *Mictlantecuhtli*, God of Death!" He spoke now only in Nahuatl. "I will guide you to him!" Felix reached back and grasped one of the long steel chaining pins Graciella had used for the perimeter flagging. He yanked it out, its bright orange ribbon trailing behind.

She sneered. "From whence *you* come, slice of maggot-ridden entrails!" Graciella, left hand on her hip, right fist raised in obscene defiance, spat her words in Nahuatl as well. Fire burned in her eyes. The transformation was completed.

"Now taste the bloody discharge from your belly, Whore of Hell!"
and, as he shouted, thrust the steel and lunged.
She swiftly stepped aside and swept her arm across, deflecting.
His inertia, now unchecked, propelled him past.
"The ez-tzotl will be yours!" she snapped, "and from your belly, oozing,
it will send a stench to comfort you in Hell!"
She turned to face him as he rose, the kiva now behind her
and the day's last light, in crimson, capped the ridge.
He crouched, both hands together, with the weapon aimed and pointing.
His snarl now came in pulsed and rapid breathing.
"Now, Offal of the Ocelot!" he growled, "You and your kiva
may together die!" He lept upon her, screaming.

She went down on her back the instant that he came upon her, and raised
her legs together
as he fell.
Up to his groin her legs struck swiftly, carried him above, beyond her.
Anger turned to terror in his yell.
The impact was behind her, dull and muted by his scream, and
the kiva roof, collapsing with his weight,
sent out protesting creaks as, one by one, the vigas splintered.
And their burden, unsupported, fell inside.
The earth beneath her trembled, then began a violent shaking,
and she lay there—felt the tremors, felt
the air itself vibrating with the shocks that rose like ripples. . .
Ripples in the lake, expanding, in concentric circles
growing
as she watched them.
"Graciella," came the softening voice that called her.
"Graciella, dearest sister. . . ."
"Yes," she answered. "Yes," more softly. "It is done, my little sister."
Stillness, now, except for calls of birds sent rudely from their slumber,
circling round their trees and calling. . . . "It is over, Xochiquetzal,
flower-Quetzal, you may rest now." Squeezing tears from weary eyelids,
feeling warmth from steady heartbeat, Graciella sighed and murmured,
"How I've missed you, sweetest sister. . .keep my love. . .my heart. . .remember."

"Graciella!" A harsh light on her face. She moved her hand towards it. "Graciella!" Someone grasping her hand. She opened her eyes and the light moved from them. Ben knelt over her. She smiled weakly. "Ben," she said. He pulled her to him, holding her close. "My God!" he said, rocking her. "Are you hurt, Graciella?"

"I'm okay, Ben," she blinked. "I'm okay. Help me up." They stood, Ben with his arm around her. Circling blue and yellow lights from a police car illuminated the surrounding trees in a silent, pulsing circuit of color. "The Lujan boys," she said. "Are they. . ."

"They're all right, Graciella," he said. He directed his flashlight on them, standing a few yards back. They looked at her, eyes wide in disbelief, afraid to come closer. Pete Montoya and another officer stood next to them, also staring at Graciella.

"Luis. Jorgé," Graciella said to them. "Are you both. . .did you see. . .?"

"They saw nothing, Graciella," Ben said. "They were unconscious when we arrived. So were you."

Graciella turned to him. "How. . .how long have I been. . .?

"You've been out for at least eight, ten minutes, Graciella," he replied. "Other than your hands, no obvious injuries. It was like you were sleeping and wouldn't awaken." He cupped her head against him. "I'm so sorry! We came too late!"

"No, Ben," Graciella looked up at him. "You didn't know! None of us did." She separated from him, turning towards the kiva. "Felix, is he. . .?"

"Dead," Ben said. He put his light beam down into the kiva. Felix lay on his back in the center, with broken vigas angling down towards him, surrounded by rubble. His eyes were open, glassy, lifeless, an expression of terror frozen on his face. Projecting from his chest was the steel chaining pin, its bright orange tape still attached.

Graciella stared at the body grimly. What force he had possessed! What overwhelming power! Gained from somewhere, deep in the past. *Her* past. Were the two of them rivals, engaged in a final combat to secure that past? She closed her eyes and turned away.

"Graciella, can you remember anything?" Ben asked. "What happened? How did Felix. . .?

"I'm. . .not sure, Ben," Graciella said. She felt it slipping away. She put her hands over her face, straining to recall. "I remember the ground shaking, birds calling. . .a lake. . .growing ripples." She shook her head as if to clear out cobwebs and dust motes. "Terrible anger. . .in a strange language. . .and Felix lunging at me with the. . .and then falling, falling, into the kiva. . . ." her voice trailed off. It was gone. The memory, the power, the authority of the incident quietly disappeared. She sensed a door closing.

"Let's leave this place," Ben said. He put his arm around her as the six of them followed the flashing circulating lights down the mound. "I don't think I can leave you alone again, Graciella," he told her. She smiled up at him and put her arm around his waist. The flashing lights were turned off, and in the surrounding blackness a sky filled with tiny lights compelled her vision. She stopped the two of them a moment and stared upward, trembling yet feeling a sudden elation, thinking about a little sister, and wondering why she couldn't remember.

23

It was Sunday morning, almost noon, when Graciella stirred in her bed, not yet fully awake. Memories of last night tumbled about in her head, uncoordinated. Flashing police lights, Felix's body, expressions of dismay and concern from her friends, all danced in a slow and random pattern across the landscape just below consciousness. She turned, clutching the pillow, and it was the pain that brought her to the surface. Her hands. She pulled them out and looked at them. Bandaged and sore, but no longer throbbing, they had been dressed by Maria as the others gathered around.

She lay in her bed, gently holding her hands palm-up by her sides, and reflected on last night. She and Ben had encountered a small crowd at the chalet as they left the grisly scene, and Ben had asked Maria and the others to return to the Center with Graciella, see to her injuries, and await him there. He had then returned to the site.

Graciella could explain only that Felix was dead, having fallen into the kiva through its unstable roof. She was a bit uncertain how her hands had become lacerated, but she was exhausted and in shock. She remembered Maria insisting that she go to bed. Maria had given her a sedative and brought her here, and she must have slept soundly, for she remembered nothing more.

A light knock on the door. Graciella sat up as the door opened cautiously, revealing Maria with a basket and carafe.

"Come in, Maria," Graciella sat up in bed.

"Good morning, Graciella," Maria put the basket on the table. "I've brought some breakfast rolls and hot tea for us." She fetched cups from the counter. "How do you feel?"

"Hands are a bit sore," she held them up, "but I slept well. Tea and rolls should bring me back to normal."

Maria gave her an ironic smile at the double meaning of the phrase, pouring tea for both of them. They sat at the table by the window and Maria adjusted the shutters to let in slivers of the bright morning light.

"Ben called a while ago," Maria said. "He's coming out to see you around twelve-thirty. He said not to eat lunch."

Graciella brightened. "Maybe just one roll, then," she said, reaching for one. "He was really frightened for me last night."

"It must have been a horrible experience for you!"

"I wish I could remember, Maria," she said. "Most of what happened is really fuzzy." She looked at her hands. Each palm had a surgical sponge dressing held on with tape. She wiggled her free fingers. "I think I remember swinging a piece of timber at Felix."

Maria took one of Graciella's hands, probing gently around the dressing. "Was this another. . .journey beyond?"

"Yes, Maria, but for the first time, I can't recall the details."

"And these wounds, Graciella? Are they still. . .?"

"Yes. They are not healed." She sighed, resting her hands on the table. "I think. . .I think, when the danger passed, so did my role on the other side."

Maria smiled at her and said, softly, "Don't you mean your obsession? To cling to that part of reality?"

"No, Maria. The obsession was the urgency of clearing the pathway from the past. It's cleared. That gate is unlocked."

"Felix had the key?"

Graciella sat in thought for a moment. "I believe Felix represented the forces that kept the path closed," she said. "The same forces he thought he was battling."

"He battled them at Picuris, too," Maria said. "Last night, Ben described Felix's dark history there. Did you know he was Picuris?" She recounted what Ben had told them after Graciella had gone to bed.

"He was misled, Maria," Graciella said. "He understood that, once opened, that passage would allow evil to come through from the past. He was wrong. While closed, it allowed the past to be hostage to those forces."

Graciella leaned forward. "Those forces were not evil in themselves, Maria," she said. "They were simply the oppressive domination of the spirit by an Aztec tradition that brought demand for obedience. An imported ritual life of sacrifice and violence, insinuated methodically into a more stoic culture. A syncretism, a new synthesis, of the kachina cult and the cult of Tlaloc finally found my people caught in its cycle."

She smiled ironically. "Either the ritual, performed correctly, or the death of Felix, would have been sufficient to release that hold and break that ancient pattern, I believe. Unfortunately, Anita died performing that ritual. Felix feared, wrongly, that the Lujan brothers were stepping in to take her place. Had he left it alone, he—his controlling spirit—would have kept their control. His death, you see, was an ironic sacrifice to that liberation."

"And now you are free," Maria said.

Graciella took a sip of her tea and thought about that statement. "Maybe that's the final irony, Maria," she replied. "I always was, I think, free of *them*. But those in the *past*. . .the people of Pot Creek Pueblo. . . *they* are now free." She paused. "Maybe I was simply the equivalent of Charon, transporting souls out of the past to the present to provide a stronger link." Her eyes flashed, "But I will never know any more about that!"

Maria got up and rinsed her cup in the sink, letting Graciella's last statement hang in the air. Graciella, too, sat quietly, the sun etching the familiar hachured design through the partially closed shutters onto the table.

When the cup was dried, Maria turned to her. "That's an interesting explanation, Graciella," she said, finally. "It might even be true, given the obvious links you have had with that past." She came back to the table, looking at Graciella. "But that isn't what I meant."

"I know, Maria," Graciella looked up at her. Held captive by her own childhood, she thought of the guilt, the unworthiness she had felt, now erased. Maria knew, after all. "Thank you."

◇◇◇

It was just after one o'clock when Ben picked her up. He had food in two saddle-bags between them in the cab of his pick-up. A quiet picnic, he told her, seemed in order after the six days of turmoil she had experienced. Refreshed and unburdened, Graciella thought so, too. She rested her hand on the darkened old leather of the saddlebags.

"Just where are we going, sir?" she asked lightly, "Or is it a surprise?"

"We've had enough surprises, I think," Ben said. "Horseback riding." He glanced at her. "You do ride?"

She nodded, smiling. "In Weatherford," she said, "one does ride." Her childhood love for horses re-entered her memory. "You've read Lonesome Dove? Charlie Goodnight is buried there. We once followed the Goodnight-Loving trail on horseback." But she had not been in a saddle for a number of years, which she would never reveal. "Where are we riding?"

Ben gave her a wink. "Blue Lake," he said. "I met with Tony and the Governor this morning. Talked with the Lujan brothers. They figure you saved their lives last night. I figure you did, too. They owe you for that, wanted to know how to thank you. I thought maybe a quiet visit to the sacred lake, just the two of us. The Governor agreed, but had to get the Tribal Council's approval." Ben half smiled without looking at her. "Be my way of redemption, too," he said. "For not being there in time."

Graciella put her hand on his shoulder and said, "You don't owe me, Ben. Any more than I owe you. But thanks."

◇◇◇

Sunlight sparkled from the lake as they brought their horses down among the trees, a single wisp of cloud trailing off the mountain above. In a clearing to the left, on a rise just above the shore, they unsaddled the horses and tied them within reach of some mountain grass. Ben spread a large wool blanket beneath a spruce while Graciella set food out. She found a bottle of wine in the pack and he opened it, pouring it in plastic cups.

They sat, eating, talking about the night before. Graciella still could not remember many details. "Ben," she asked, "do you remember feeling the ground shaking? Like an earthquake?"

"You mentioned that last night," he said. "No. There was nothing like that. I asked Luis and Jorge, but they were at best semi-conscious when I arrived. No one felt anything."

"I'm sure I felt it," she said. "I can't understand why my memory has failed."

"You were pretty well traumatized," Ben said. "Maybe it's temporary."

Graciella leaned back on her elbows and looked out over the lake. "Or maybe it's something else," she said. She turned to him. "Ben, I think it's finished. This split reality. The link between the two, whatever it was, is broken. The old kiva people, my imaginary sister, my affinity for them and their language and their way of life, they're all back there in some sheltered beginning. They won't reach for me again."

"Does that make you sad?"

"It makes me. . .comfortable. Like there's a tranquil part of me I hadn't been able to touch for a long time."

"Maybe because you no longer have to reach for *them*," Ben said.

"You're a psychologist, too," Graciella smiled.

"Just a dumb old Indian," Ben said, "who has a hard time figuring out pretty young archeologists."

On impulse, Graciella leaned over and kissed him quickly, brushing the back of her hand along his braid. She held his face in her hands, looking into his eyes. "You're doing a lot better than I am, Ben Sandoval," she said.

He smiled back at her. "There," he said. "That time I felt it. The shaking earth. Probably a four on the Richter Scale."

She laughed, turned around, and lay with her head in his lap. "Good medicine, Apache," she said. "Those were spirit drums," looking up at him and beyond, at the sweeping boughs of the spruce and the wisp of cloud and the blue sky mirrored in the blue waters below. Where a tiny ripple began slowly growing in concentric circles.

Readers Guide

1. This novel is about the line that divides "reality" into mythical and non-mythical segments. The term "myth" here has two meanings—one is a story that involves (but is not restricted to) the supernatural; the other is a belief that is untrue. Which of the definitions would divide "myth" from "reality" as two separate entities? When Graciella first experiences the strange phenomenon in Room 703, what is her initial definition of the experience? Throughout the story, how does her definition change?

2. Graciella is training to be a scientist. How does her training interfere with her assessment of her experiences? Since she is surrounded by fellow-scientists, she is reluctant to share both her experiences and her interpretations of them. Can you think of real-life circumstances which mirror these feelings?

3. In this novel a parallel line divides the subconscious from the conscious—particularly "dreaming" from "wakefulness." In Graciella's case, is she the same person on both sides of this line? What childhood experience leads her to accept a duality of identity?

4. Throughout her extra-normal episodes, a sensory experience always accompanies her transition. What is this? What ancient meanings do these organic objects represent—and how realistic are these meanings? Think about the several healing dimensions of folk medicine: emotional, psychological, and physical. Compare this with Western medicine.

5. Detective Sandoval helps Graciella resolve the duality dilemma. How does he do this? Does his Native American ancestry play a role in this resolution?

6. The story intentionally resists an explicit affirmation or denial of this duality. Does this help to convey an understanding of Graciella's ambiguity?

7. Graciella never fears or feels apprehensive about her "contact" with the "other side," yet she grows increasingly fearful of a personal danger that results from this contact. Do you think this set of contrasting emotions is logical? How can this be explained?

8. There is evidence in the story that evil and good can apply to both persons and places. Can you think of actual examples? Both of these do not necessarily involve the paranormal, yet both may be rationally appraised and, perhaps, explained. How is this addressed in the novel? Do you think the person v. place difference is reconcilable?

9. At the conclusion of the story, Graciella asserts that her connection with the parallel reality has finally been severed, as abruptly as it began. There are several events that may have contributed to this feeling on her part. What are they?

10. One of the central themes in the novel is that, just as the past influences the present, the present can also influence the past. There are obviously some mystical explanations for this, but are there realistic and historical explanations as well? In what ways, in the story, is the connection between past and present both non-linear and time-independent?

11. The story uses prosody (rhythm, syllabic stress)—but not rhyme—to reflect dialogue from the alternative (parallel?) reality when in contact with Graciella. In this case, meter plays a central role in narrative. This is characteristic of oral transmission, in particular where no written language prevails. It thus serves a dual purpose, both reflecting the meaning imbedded in the transmission and the meaning received by the listener (or, in this case, the reader). Many original pre-writing epics occur in this form, in large part to foster memory. Can you find some examples?